Richard Laymon was born in Chicago in 1947. He grew up in California and has a BA in English Literature from Williamette University, Oregon, and an MA from Loyola University, Los Angeles. He has worked as a school-teacher, a librarian and as a report writer for a law firm. He now works full time as a writer. Apart from his novels, he has published more than sixty short stories in magazines such as *Ellery Queen, Alfred Hitchcock* and *Cavalier* and in anthologies, including *Modern Masters of Horror, The Second Black Lizard Anthology of Crime* and *Night Visions 7*. His novel *Flesh* ws named Best Horror novel of 1988 by *Science Fiction Chronicle* and also listed for the prestigious Bram Stoker Award, as was *Funland*. Richard Laymon is the author of more than twenty acclaimed novels, including *The Cellar, The Stake, Savage, Quake, Island, Body Rides, Bite* and *Fiends*. He lives in California with his wife and daughter.

For Richard Laymon fan club information, readers may contact Martin White c/o The Ramoy Business Centre, 4 Broomfields Street, Paisley PA1 2LR. E-mail: Ramoybc@aol.com, fax: 0141 848 6669. For up-to-date cyberspace news of Richard Laymon and his books, contact Richard Laymon Kills! at: http://www.crafti.com.au/~gerlach/rlaymon.htm

The Woods Are Dark

Richard Laymon

HEADLINE
FEATURE

First published in paperback in Great Britain in 1983
by New English Library

Reprinted in this edition in 1991 by
HEADLINE BOOK PUBLISHING

A HEADLINE FEATURE paperback

20 19 18 17 16 15 14

ISBN 0 7472 3550 3

Typeset by Medcalf Type Ltd, Bicester
Printed and bound in Great Britain by
Mackays of Chatham plc, Chatham, Kent

HEADLINE BOOK PUBLISHING
A division of Hodder Headline PLC
338 Euston Road
London NW1 3BH

The Woods Are Dark

Chapter One

Neala O'Hare slowed her MG as the narrow road
curved. The evening sun was no longer behind
her. Shadows of the high trees threw their dark
capes across the road, hiding it. She pulled off her
sunglasses.

'Here, would you stow these in the glove
compartment?'

Sherri, in the passenger seat, took the glasses.
She opened the glove compartment. 'Christ, I'm
starving. You don't suppose we'll run into a
McDonalds?'

'I've got some gorp in my pack.'

'Gorp? Thanks anyway. I'd rather . . . ' She
suddenly gasped.

Neala saw it, too. She hit the brakes.

Her friend thrust a hand against the windshield
as the car jerked to a stop.

In front of them, the legless thing dragged itself
over the road with powerful, hairy arms.

'What the fuck *is* it?' Sherri muttered.

Neala shook her head.

Then it faced them.

Neala's hands clenched the steering wheel.
Stunned, she tried to figure out what she was

seeing. It hardly looked like the face of a man.

The thing turned. It started to drag itself toward the car.

'Get out of here!' Sherri cried. 'Quick! Back up!'

'What *is* it?' Neala asked.

'Let's *go*!'

Neala backed up, but slowly, just enough to keep away from the approaching creature. She couldn't take her eyes off its bloated face.

'Run it over!' Sherri snapped.

She shook her head. 'I can't. It's a man. I think it's a man.'

'Who cares? For Godsake, run it over and let's get the fuck out of here!'

It sat up, balancing on its torso, freeing its arms. It leered at Neala.

'Oh God,' Sherri muttered.

It fumbled at an opening in its furry vest. A pocket? It pulled out a severed human hand, kissed its palm, and tossed it. The hand flipped toward Neala. She ducked her head, felt it in her hair, and knocked it aside. It fell into the gap between the bucket seats.

The legless thing scuttled off the road and disappeared into the forest.

Neala looked down at the hand, at its crooked fingers, its coral painted nails, the white band of skin where a wedding ring used to be. Lunging sideways, she threw herself over her door and vomited onto the pavement. When she was done, she turned to her friend.

'We've gotta get rid of it,' Sherri said.

'I . . .'

Snarling as if enraged, Sherri clutched the hand by its fingers and flung it from the car. 'God!' She rubbed her hand furiously on her shorts.

Neala sped away.

As she drove, her mind repeated the incident again and again. She needed to make sense of it, but no matter how she concentrated, it wouldn't fall into a pattern she could accept. The scene belonged in a nightmare, not on a peaceful road on the way to Yosemite.

She was glad to see a town ahead – not much of a town, to be sure. Up in these areas, though, they rarely were.

'Maybe they've got a police department,' she said.

'You're not planning to stop!'

'We ought to tell somebody.'

'Tell Father Higgins, for Godsake. Save it for confession. Jesus, let's get the hell out of here.'

'We can't just forget about it.'

'Forget about it? Every time I shut my eyes, I'm going to be looking into that repulsive, gloating . . .' Sherri jerked her head sharply as if to shake the picture apart. 'God, I'm *never* gonna forget about it. But we don't have to go around making a big deal of it, okay? Let's just keep it to ourselves. It's water over the dam, you know?'

They had already left half the town behind. Ahead of them, Neala saw a bait shop, Terk's Diner, and the Sunshine Motor Inn.

'Why don't we stop at the diner?' Neala suggested.

'Let's not.'

'Come on. It's late. You just said you're starving.'

'I lost my appetite.'

'Please. I'd sure like to get out of the car and relax, at least. Try to think it out. Talk it over. Besides, there's no telling when we'll hit another restaurant.'

'You call this a restaurant?'

'Hey, this is your kind of joint. Probably filthy with greasy spoons and "characters." '

Sherri managed a smile. 'Okay. But let's keep the freak to ourselves.'

Neala turned onto the gravel parking area, and shut down the engine. 'Let's batten down the hatches,' Neala said. 'It'll be dark when we get out.' They latched the roof into place, rolled up the windows, and locked the doors. Before starting across the gravel, Neala stretched.

She was stiff from the long day in the car. Standing on tiptoes, shoulders straining back, she felt the luxury of her tensing muscles. The movement pulled her shirt taut across her chest. She liked its feel against her nipples, and thought how long it had been since she'd felt the eager touch of a man's fingers or tongue on her breasts.

Maybe, up in Yosemite, she'd get lucky.

Meet a rugged Mountain Man.

One for Sherri, too. I'm not selfish.

'I feel almost human again,' she said, meeting Sherri behind the car.

They crossed the gravel lot to the entrance of the diner. Sherri pulled open the screen door, and they walked in.

Neala liked the warmth. The familiar aromas

made her long for a cheeseburger and French fries. 'Counter?' she asked, seeing a pair of empty stools at the end. The other half a dozen were occupied.

'Let's take a table,' Sherri said, surprising her. Sherri usually preferred the counter, where she struck up conversations with nearby strangers.

Not tonight, apparently.

They slid into booths at a side table, facing each other. Sherri's eyes briefly met Neala's, then lowered.

'Buck up, pardner,' Neala said.

'Sure thing.'

'Don't be this way. Please.'

'Oh, how should I be?'

'Be the gutsy champ we all know and admire.'

That didn't even get a smile from Sherri.

Neala needed that smile. She'd never felt so stunned, so alone. This was a hell of a time for Sherri to go silent and glum.

'Would it help if I apologize?' Neala asked.

'It's not your fault.'

'It was my idea to go backpacking.'

'The freak wasn't your idea.'

'That's for damn sure. But if we'd stayed home . . .'

'It's all right. Forget it.'

The waitress came. 'Sorry to keep you folks waiting,' she said. She set water glasses on the table, and handed out menus.

When she left, they studied the menus. Usually, they would talk over the offerings, maybe decide to split an order of fries or onion rings, discuss whether to 'blow it' and have milk shakes. Tonight, they kept silence.

Neala picked at a speck of yellow food on the menu, then wished she hadn't touched it.

The waitress returned. 'Ready to order?'

Neala nodded. 'I'll have one of your Terkburger Specials and iced tea.' She watched the gaunt, unsmiling woman write it down.

Can't anyone smile tonight? she wondered.

This gal ought to be happy as a lark, with a ring like that on her pinky.

'A patty melt,' Sherri said. 'Fries, and a Pepsi.'

The woman nodded. She took the menus, and walked away.

Sherri watched her, frowning.

'Did you get a load of her ring?' Neala asked, hoping to break the somber mood.

'How could I miss it? The thing nearly blinded me.'

'Do you suppose it was glass?'

'Looked real enough to me. I'm no expert, though. Besides, I left my jeweler's loop at home.'

Neala laughed, and saw the hint of a smile on Sherri's face. 'It looked like a wedding ring,' she said.

'Wrong finger. Wrong hand, too. She probably outgrew it.'

'Her? She was nothing but bones.'

'Maybe it's a friendship ring,' Sherri suggested. 'I could use a friend like that. Money coming out his wazoo. If I were that gal, I'd blow this burg in about two seconds. Grab hold of the guy, and light out for the big city.'

6

When the waitress brought their supper, they both watched her hand.

'What do you think?' Neala asked when she was gone.

'I think it's real.'

Neala bit into her Terkburger: a thick patty on a sesame seed bun. Juice spilled down her chin. She back-handed it off, and reached for a napkin. 'Delicious,' she said.

'Same here,' said Sherri. Strings of limp onion dangled from the sides of her sandwich.

'Onion breath.'

'You planning to kiss me?' Sherri asked.

'Not tonight.'

'Gee whiz, and I had my heart set on it.'

'You're sure going to stink up the tent. Maybe we'd better sleep under the stars.'

'What if it rains?' Sherri asked through a mouthful that muffled her words.

'Then we get wet.'

'I wouldn't like that.'

'Better than onion gas in the tent.'

'Yeah?' Sherri pulled off the top slab of rye bread, pinched a matted glob of onions, and dropped it onto Neala's plate. 'You have some, too. Insurance.'

Laughing, Neala piled the onions onto her Terkburger and ate.

Soon, their plates were empty. Neala thought about returning to the car. She didn't want to.

'How about dessert?' Sherri asked, as if she were in no hurry to leave, either.

'Good idea.'

This was no time to worry about calories. Neala never worried much about them, regardless; she had no trouble keeping her trim figure. Still, gloppy desserts made her guilty. Tonight, it would be worth the guilt to postpone returning to the car.

They both ordered hot fudge sundaes. They ate slowly, picking at the mounds of ice cream, the thick warm syrup, the whipped cream sprinkled with chopped nuts.

'This'll add an inch to my hips,' Sherri said. She was several inches taller than Neala, with broad shoulders, prominent breasts, and big hips. She wasn't fat, but an additional inch on her hips wouldn't be that noticeable. Neala decided to keep the observation to herself.

'We'll work it all off, this week,' she said.

'A great way to spend a vacation, working our asses off.'

'You'll love it.'

'Sure I will. I'll love it plenty if Robert Redford wanders over to our campfire and I bowl him over with my wit and charm, and he drags me off with him. My luck, though, he'd fall for you.'

'I'd share.'

'Promise?'

When the sundaes were gone, they ordered coffee.

After this, Neala thought, we'll have to go. Back to the car. Back to the narrow, dark road and the woods.

We can't stay here all night.

She watched the waitress shut the main, wooden door. Through the window, she saw that dusk had fallen. The gravel of the parking lot was a gray blur. Across the road, the sign of the Sunshine Motor Inn blinked gloomy blue. It showed a vacancy.

Her eyes met Sherri's.

'No way,' Sherri said.

'I know. I don't want to stay, either. I don't want to go and I don't want to stay.'

'We'll feel a lot better when we've put some miles behind us.'

Neala nodded agreement.

'But before we do another thing, the kid here's gonna hit the john.'

While she was gone, Neala had another cup of coffee.

She came back, and Neala went. The toilet, at the rear of the diner, was clean and pleasant. Ought to be, Neala thought; the place is run by a bunch of tycoons.

She returned to the table. Sherri had already put down the tip. They took the bill to the cash register. This meal was Neala's turn.

She bought two foil-wrapped mints for the road.

The waitress poured change into her hand. 'Don't be strangers,' she said.

Sherri reached for the knob, and tried to turn it. The knob didn't move. She tried again. 'Hey, Miss?' she called to the waitress.

The heads of everyone at the counter turned toward them.

'Hey Miss, the door's stuck.'

The customers stared. A couple of the younger ones smiled, but most looked grim.

9

'Ain't stuck, honey. It's locked.'

Neala felt a tight pull of fear in her bowels.

'How about *un*locking it?' Sherri asked.

'Afraid I can't do that.'

'Yeah? Why the fuck not?'

''Cause you're here to stay, you two.'

With a big grin, the waitress turned to the other customers – the same customers, Neala suddenly realized, who'd been at the counter when they entered, so long ago.

Silently, four of the men climbed off their stools.

Chapter Two

Lander Dills cut his high beams as a car appeared around a bend. When it was gone, he pressed them on again, doubling the brightness of the road and forest ahead.

'This is the forest primeval,' he announced. 'The murmuring pines and the hemlocks.'

'That's Dad doing his *Evangeline* routine,' said Cordelia in the back seat, explaining him to Ben. 'He gets poetically inspired at frequent intervals.'

'Fine with me,' Ben said.

Good fellow, Ben. Didn't know an iamb from a dactyl, and couldn't care less, but at least he seemed reasonably intelligent and polite. Lander, a high school teacher, had seen enough of the other kind to last him a dozen lifetimes.

His daughter had good taste in boyfriends, thank the gods.

'Longfellow knew his stuff,' Lander said. 'The forest primeval. You can feel it in your bones – the silence, the isolation. Out there, nothing has changed for a thousand years. "Down by the dank tarn of Auber, in the ghoul-haunted woodland of Weir." '

'The Poe routine,' Cordelia said.

'I wouldn't mind his motel routine, about now,' said Ruth.

'Mom's horny, too.'

'That's not what I meant, Cordie, and you know it!'

Cordelia and Ben were laughing. The motel routine. With a pang, Lander pictured his daughter under Ben, naked and moaning. From the way the two acted, he was certain they had gone the whole route. It made him feel sick, as if he'd lost something precious. She was eighteen, though. Old enough to know what she was doing, to make her own choices. He couldn't stop her. He wouldn't try. But it hurt him.

'We should be coming into a Barlow pretty soon,' Ruth said, shining her flashlight at a roadmap on her lap. 'How about stopping there?'

'Don't you want to try for Mule Ear Lake?' Lander asked.

'We're *hours* away, honey. It'll be midnight, at least, and we told Mr Elsworth we'd be there by nine. He'll probably be asleep. Besides, we've been on the road all day.'

'If we *had* been on the road all day, we'd be there by now.'

'Here we go,' Cordelia said. 'The general. His idea of a vacation is hitting the road before sun-up.'

'Well, I'd be happy to stay in Barlow, myself,' he said. 'I'm just looking out for you people.' He grinned through the darkness at Ruth. 'You do realize, I hope, there won't be a Hyatt.'

'As long as we have clean sheets . . .'

'Would you kids rather stop, or go on through to the cabin?'

'Let's stop,' Cordelia said. 'It'll be fun.'

'Either way's fine with me, Mr Dills.'

'Well, we'll see,' he said.

He wouldn't argue the point. Not worth the trouble. He was pleased enough to assume the role of leader, but only so long as nobody tampered with his decisions. His decision, from the start, had been to drive on through. Now, he'd been over-ruled.

With some satisfaction, and telling nobody, he switched his role from leader to chauffeur.

If they want to run the show, let them. He would sit back, relieved of responsibility, and watch. More than likely, they would botch it.

Soon, he came to the town of Barlow. He drove past a closed gas station, a general store, Phillips' Hardware. Just ahead, on the right, was Terk's Diner. Across the road was the Sunshine Motor Inn. Its flashing blue sign read, 'Vacancy.'

'Is this where you want to stop?' he asked, slowing down. It wasn't a regular motel, at all, but a cluster of cottages behind a shabby office. A motor court.

'I don't know,' Ruth said. She sounded dubious. Lander grinned.

'What do you think?' she asked him.

'It's up to you. Should we give it a try?'

'What do you think, kids?' Ruth asked.

'I don't know,' said Cordelia. 'It looks kind of creepy, to me.'

Lander stopped the car in the middle of the

13

road. He waited, watching his rear-view mirror in case a car should come along.

'Shall we?' Ruth asked him.

'If you want to.'

'You're a lot of help,' she complained.

'Give the word, and we'll stay here.'

'Okay,' Ruth said. 'Let's give it a try.'

Flipping on his turn signal, Lander drove across the road and stopped beside the lighted office. 'You might as well wait in here.'

'Hold it,' Ruth said. 'What are you going to do?'

'Register.'

'You know what I mean.'

'I don't think we can all fit in one of these hovels, do you?'

She shook her head.

'So I'll get two. Boys in one, girls in the other.'

'Oh *Dad*!'

'No,' he said. 'I'm perfectly willing to spend the night here, if that's what everyone wants, but I won't sponsor your sexual escapades.'

'Lander!'

'God, Dad!'

'That was uncalled for,' Ruth said.

He'd expected a showdown over the sleeping arrangements for the trip. He should have handled it beforehand, but he'd hoped to avoid it, somehow. 'I'm sorry,' he said, 'but that's how I feel. As long as we're all together, they won't be sharing a bedroom. Not here, and not at the cabin.'

'That's great,' Cordelia muttered. 'Just great.'

'It's either that, or I turn this buggy around and we call the whole thing off.'

'That's fine with me,' Cordelia said.

'It's not fine with me,' said Ruth. 'We came up here for a good time, and that's what were going to have. I happen to agree with your father. We never allowed Ben to spend the night with you at home, and I don't see any reason to start now, simply because we're on vacation. If you were married, it would be a different kettle of fish, but . . .'

'Marriage. A license to screw.'

'If you think that,' Lander said, 'you've got a lot more growing up to do.'

'I agree with your parents,' Ben said.

'Thanks a bunch.'

'Not about growing up. I mean, you know.'

Cordelia sighed. 'What's this, gang up on Cordie night?'

'I'll get the rooms,' Lander said. He was glad to leave the car, and the argument.

Bells jingled as he entered the office. He waited several moments at the deserted counter. Then a door opened, off to the side. A man came out of the dimly lighted room beyond. The door started to swing shut, but stopped, leaving a three-inch gap. Half a face appeared behind the gap, looking out at Lander with a single eye.

'Room?' asked the man. He seemed pleasant enough. Chubby and bald, with a cherubic smile, he looked like he should be doing skits on a television comedy show.

'Uh, yes,' Lander said. 'Two rooms.'

The eye behind the door watched him, only a slit of it showing through the fleshy lid.

15

'There are four of us. Do you have connecting rooms?'

'Nothing like that, sorry. We can put you all up in one room, though, if you want. We've got one, sleeps three. We can wheel in an extra bed.'

'No, that's all right. Do you have two rooms available?'

'Sure do.' He smiled. 'Want to fill out a guest registration card?'

As Lander filled in the requested information, his hand shook slightly. That person in the doorway . . .

Twice, he looked up. The face was still pressed to the crack. It was an ancient face. He couldn't tell whether it belonged to a man or woman. The eye blinked, dripping fluid from its corners.

He finished the card, and handed it back along with his MasterCard.

The man ran it through the machine. 'That'll be $42.50 for the rooms. One night. Check out time is noon. Want to sign here?'

Lander signed the bill.

He looked up at the door. It was shut.

'All set, Mr Dills.' The man bent down and came up with two keys. 'That's bungalows three and twelve.'

'Are they close together?'

'Well, one's just behind the office here. The other's back a ways.'

'Do you have any that aren't so far apart?'

'It's the best I can do for you, Mr Dills. We've got a pretty good crowd, tonight.'

'Okay. That'll be fine. Thanks.'

16

'Enjoy your stay with us.'

Lander nodded. He pulled open the door and stepped outside, relieved to get away from the office.

He climbed into the car.

'Well?' Ruth asked.

'Got 'em. Three and twelve.' His hand hesitated on the ignition key.

What's wrong?'

'Nothing, I guess. Probably the guy's mother.'

'What?'

'Some old buzzard kept watching me while I was in there. It spooked me a bit. She – he – whatever, kept staring at me through a crack in the door.'

'Dad!' Cordelia sounded frightened.

'I'm sure she's perfectly harmless,' Ruth said.

'Yeah,' said Lander. He started the car, and drove slowly into the dark courtyard, taking some comfort from the presence of the other cars parked nearby, glad his family wasn't alone at this God-awful motel.

Chapter Three

As two men held Neala from behind, the waitress took her purse and tossed it onto the counter. A teenaged girl grabbed it, and started looking through its contents.

'She's got cool shoes,' said a freckled boy beside the girl. 'Let's see 'em.'

'They won't fit you,' the girl said.

'Might. 'Sides, she don't need 'em.'

The waitress knelt, and pulled off one of Neala's running shoes. Neala didn't try to stop the woman. The last time she'd protested, one of the men had bent her arm backwards. Sherri, who'd given them a rough time at first, got punched in the stomach for her trouble. Neala figured she would let them have whatever they wanted, and hope for the best.

The waitress tossed the shoes to the boy. He caught them, and climbed onto the counter to try them on.

Neala's wristwatch went next. Then her school ring from Loyola-Marymount. The waitress dropped them into her apron pocket, where they clinked in the loose change from her tips. Her rough hands tugged the neck of Neala's old workshirt. The top button popped off and skittered across the floor. Normally, she wore a gold chain necklace. She was glad she'd left it home for the backpacking trip.

The woman flicked the hair away from Neala's ears, mumbled about finding no earrings, and slapped her.

Then she sidestepped and repeated the process with Sherri, taking her purse, her sandals, her two rings. Sherri had no watch, but her crucifix hung by a gold chain at her throat. The waitress carefully opened the clasp, then dropped the chain into her apron pocket. Sherri cried out, squirming in the arms of the two big men as the waitress ripped the gold loop earrings from her pierced lobes.

'That it?' asked one of the men holding Sherri.

'Guess so,' the waitress said.

Neala heard a metallic rattle. Her left arm was jerked down. A handcuff hit her wrist. It latched shut with a quick ratchet sound. The second cuff locked around Sherri's wrist.

'Okay ladies, let's go.'

Someone pushed Sherri. She stumbled forward, snapping the chain taut, tugging Neala's cuff. The sharp edges bit into Neala's wrist. She lurched forward, trying to stay close to Sherri so it wouldn't happen again.

'I'm going along,' the freckled boy said.

'Pervert,' said the girl.

He jumped down from the counter, wearing Neala's shoes, and raced to the rear door of the diner. He held it open while the men guided Sherri through, then Neala.

'Where are you taking us?' Sherri asked. She sounded, to Neala, remarkably calm.

The men didn't answer. From the start, they'd said very little. All four stayed quiet and solemn, as if carrying out an unpleasant necessity.

The boy ran ahead of them. At the rear of an old pickup truck, he tried to open the tailgate. He was still working on it, without success, when one of the men arrived and gave him a hand. Together, they dropped the gate. It fell with a clamor that resounded in the night's stillness.

The boy scampered onto the truck bed. The man walked to the cab. As he climbed in, the others pushed Neala and Sherri toward the pickup's rear gate.

'This is kidnapping, you know,' Sherri told them.

'That's the least of your troubles, sister.'

They were tugged and lifted onto the metal floor of the truck bed. A man on the ground swung up the gate. It crashed into place. He latched it, climbed aboard, and sat down at Neala's feet.

The truck started to move, lurching over the rutted lot. Neala's head banged the floor. She lifted it.

'Stay down,' said the man beside her.

After a turn and a final sharp bounce, the truck steadied out.

We're on the highway, Neala realized. Heading west. Back the way we came.

'Where are you taking us?' Sherri asked.

'Not far,' said the man beside her.

'You're going to kill us, aren't you?'

The question made Neala's stomach hurt. Why couldn't Sherri keep her mouth shut!

'Not us,' the man said.

'I want to check them out,' said the boy.

'Help yourself.'

'For Christsake, Shaw,' said the man beside Neala.

'Ah, let the kid,' argued the one at her feet. 'No harm done.'

'It isn't right.'

'So what the hell *is* right?'

'He's pushing twelve,' said Shaw – the boy's father? 'He needs the education.'

'Every time we get a good young one, Timmy's at her. It's disgusting.'

'Going queer, Robbins?'

'I just don't think it's right. Do you? We don't have to turn into a bunch of savages, for Christsake. Next thing you know, we'll be the ones raping and . . .'

'That ain't allowed, and you know it,' Shaw said.

'It's the next step, damn it! We let Timmy do whatever he wants, next thing you know he'll be screwing 'em.'

'No I won't,' Timmy pouted.

'He knows better than that.'

'You ever tell him what they did to Weiss?'

Silence.

'I don't want to scare you, kid, but we used to have a guy named Weiss on these runs.'

'Shut up, Robbins.'

'Weiss knew better, too. He knew the rules.'

'Robbins!'

'Let him tell,' said the man at Neala's feet. 'The kid better know, for his own good.'

'We had this really beautiful gal, about six years back. Weiss couldn't stand it. We should've stopped him. I don't know why we didn't, but I guess we were tempted, ourselves, and figured we wouldn't mind watching him. Safe enough, just watching. Anyway, he had her right here in the truck.'

'He *screwed* her?' Timmy asked. Neala heard eagerness in the boy's voice.

'A few days later, he vanished. Weiss and his whole family: his wife and three kids. They vanished in the middle of the night, right out of their home.'

'Maybe they ran away,' Timmy suggested.

'No. The Krulls got 'em.'

'How do you know?'

'We found evidence,' Shaw explained.

'So just remember Weiss, when you get an urge to start exploring our ladies here.'

'It's okay, long as I don't screw 'em.'

'Christ, kid, where are your brains?'

'Knock that off,' Shaw snapped.

'Dad can I?'

'Let him,' said the man at Neala's feet.

'Just a little?' Timmy asked.

'You want to end up like Weiss?' Robbins asked.

'Long as I don't screw 'em . . .'

'Shit,' Robbins muttered.

'We're almost there,' Shaw said. 'Go ahead, but don't dawdle.'

Timmy crawled to Sherri's head. Kneeling, he leaned over her.

'Don't touch me, kid,' she snarled. 'I'll kill you, I swear it.'

Timmy looked at his father.

'Just shut up, sister.'

'Yeah!' Timmy said. 'You're just a big ox anyway. Who'd *want* to feel you up?'

He suddenly lunged onto Neala, his belly pressing her face, his hands pulling her shirt from her waist. She felt his hands rubbing her belly, pushing under the waist of her corduroys, one reaching inside her panties and moving in deep, fingers pressing and entering her.

With her free right hand, she hammered the center of Timmy's back. He jerked with the impact. Then a spasm of coughing shook his body. His hand went away. So did the pressure of his belly on Neala's face.

'Damn it, Robbins!' Shaw shouted. 'You shouldn't have let her do that!'

'She caught me off guard.'

Timmy knelt above her, shaking as he coughed.

'Goddamn bastard,' Shaw muttered.

The boy was crying, now. He suddenly gasped, 'You!' and punched Neala's face with a small, hard fist. She flung up her arm to stop the next blow, but Robbins had already shoved Timmy. The boy tumbled backwards.

'That's enough,' Robbins said.

'Dad!'

'Nobody touches my boy pal!'

'Yeah? I do. The kid's out of hand. He's starting

to act like a shit, and I'm not going to let it go on. Not while I'm on this run.'

The man at Neala's feet said, 'What's got into you, Robbins? All the kid wanted was to cop a little feel. How come you're so touchy, all of a sudden? Last week, you were helping him. You stepped on that gal's hand, remember?'

'I don't feel so great about that, either.'

'What the fuck, did you get religion or something?'

'Something.'

The pickup lurched as it turned onto a dirt road. Overhead, the woods closed in, shutting out the moonlight.

Chapter Four

'Who's for a nightcap?' Lander asked, once they'd carried the suitcases into cottage twelve.

'You mean a Pepsi?' Cordelia asked.

'Whatever you like. Pepsi, 7-Up, hard stuff. We'll hoist a couple to fortify Ben and me for the long trek back to three.'

'Dad's trying to mollify us,' she told Ben.

Lander opened his Travel Bar. 'Vodka for me,' he said, smiling at his daughter's remark. After all, she was right. She may be a smart-aleck and over-sexed, but she wasn't stupid. 'A Manhattan?' he asked Ruth.

'That'll hit the spot.'

'What's your pleasure, Ben?'

Cordelia smirked at the boy. 'Don't get your hopes up,' she said. 'You won't be getting that, tonight.'

Lander was pleased to see Ben blush.

'Just a Pepsi, I guess.'

'We don't have any ice,' Ruth told them.

Cordelia smiled. 'I saw a machine by the office.'

'I'll go get some,' Ben volunteered.

'Good man.'

'I'll go with you,' Cordelia said. At the door, she

27

turned to Lander. 'Don't worry, Dad, we won't indulge in sexual escapades.'

They left.

Lander poured rye into one of the glasses from his case. He opened the small Vermouth bottle.

'You sure opened a can of worms,' Ruth said.

'It's Vermouth.'

She ignored his attempt at humor.

'The *can*,' Lander explained, 'was open already. I only tried to put a lid on it. Not even that, really. If they want to have at it, let them do it on the sly. It's more fun that way, anyhow. "Stolen sweets are best." '

'I don't know,' Ruth said. 'Maybe we should let them share a room. They are eighteen, you know. In a couple of months, they'll both be going off to Santa Barbara, and we won't have any say in what they do.'

'All the more reason to have our say now.'

'Over here,' Cordie whispered. She pulled Ben toward a dark path between two of the cottages.

'We'd better get the ice.'

'What's the hurry?'

'They'll be waiting.'

'Let 'em wait. Come on. This'll be our only chance to be alone, tonight.'

'Just for a minute,' Ben said. 'We don't want to get your dad angry.'

'Speak for yourself.'

'Did you really think he'd let us sleep together?'

'God no. Dad? It was worth a try, though.' She

led Ben into the shadows. Wrapping her arms around him, she lightly touched her lips to his mouth. He seemed hesitant, at first — preoccupied. She kissed him more deeply, opening her mouth, sucking his tongue into her.

Ben pulled her tightly against him, and she felt his erection against her belly. If only she were wearing a skirt instead of these tight jeans! Moaning with frustration, she rubbed against him. His leg bent. She rode his upthrust thigh, grinding herself against it, slipping a hand down the front of his pants. One of his hands went inside her blouse. It squeezed her breast through the thin sheath of her bra.

Abruptly, his whole body shook. He bit her tongue. His hand clenched, shooting pain through her breast. He pumped warm fluid into her hand, and dropped to his knees.

Behind him, hammer poised for another blow, stood a grinning, toothless old woman.

'It's sure taking them a long time,' Lander complained. He swirled his warm vodka, and sipped it.

'They haven't been alone all day.'

'You'd think they could exercise a little restraint.'

'They're in love, honey.'

'I know, I know.'

Ruth sat down on the bed beside him. 'You're not exactly the world champ at exercising restraint, yourself. Remember the night on the porch glider?'

He laughed softly. 'I thought sure your dad would catch us.'

'And how you brought a can of oil the next night?'

'I wonder if they ever noticed the squeak was gone.'

'I sure did.'

'I oiled you both that night.'

'Geez, Lander!' She gave him a playful shove.

'I noticed you stopped squeaking, too.'

'You're awful!'

They kissed. Her lips were pliant and warm and familiar. He felt the gentle pressure of her hand on his leg. 'Hey,' he said, 'we'd better not get started.'

'Better not,' she echoed. 'Guess we'll have to exercise restraint.'

'That's not what I'd like to exercise,' he said.

She pushed him, laughing. 'How about *you* getting the ice? It'll keep you out of mischief.'

'Yeah, and maybe I'll run into the love-birds.' He picked up the room key and went out the door. Outside, he tried the knob to be sure it was locked. He climbed down the wooden stairs and scanned the three small duplexes across the driveway. No sign of Cordelia or Ben. He glanced into the car. Not there.

From the middle of the dirt driveway, he had a good view of all six cottages, the office and the main road. Turning, he looked behind him. The drive ended, and the forest began.

The forest primeval. The murmuring pines and the hemlocks . . .

Maybe they went in there for a tumble in the hemlocks. Joking about it didn't help.

It's no joke, your own daughter having a tumble.

Roll me over in the clover . . .

He pictured Cordelia on her back, Ben pumping. It made his stomach hurt.

Roll me over lay me down and do it again.

I'm obsessed, he thought.

Jealous?

Crap.

Where *are* they?

Could they get into one of the cottages? He studied each, turning as he walked, sometimes walking backwards. Six duplexes. Twelve rooms in all. Lights on in the windows of about half. Cars were parked in front of several others. Real clunkers. One, he noticed – an ancient, battered Buick Special – even had a flat tire. One of its windows was down.

He shook his head. No. They wouldn't dare make out in a stranger's car.

Stopping, he eyed each car with new suspicion. Four, not counting his own. The kids could be in any of them, rutting on the back seat.

Rutting?

Shame burned Lander's face as he changed direction and walked across the dirt to the Buick. He moved close enough to see that the back seat was empty, then veered away and approached the next car.

A Maverick. Its right rear corner was badly bashed as if a metal-eating monster had taken a bite from it. Stepping closer, he glanced into the back seat. A dark shape jumped, and sprang through the far window. A cat. Lander laughed softly at his own fright. He patted his chest, where his heart pounded frantically, and looked again into the car. Baby shoes hung from the rear-view mirror. His eyes lowered to the steering column. Something weird there. With a quick glance around to be sure he wasn't being watched, he opened the passenger door and leaned across the seat.

On the steering column where the ignition should be, he saw only a round hole.

Strange, all right.

He climbed out, silently shut the door, and stepped to the front. His fingers searched beneath the lip of the hood. He found the latch and released it. He raised the hood, hinges squawking.

No battery.

No radiator, no fan belt, no carburetor, no air cleaner. The engine had been cannibalized.

'Jesus,' he muttered, and lowered the hood.

He ran across the driveway to a dilapidated Grand Prix. Raised its hood. Gazed into the darkness where the engine should have been, and found no engine at all. The car was an empty shell.

What kind of a motel was this, leaving useless cars in front of its room like – decoys?

With a sudden chill of dread, Lander wondered if the entire place was deserted: lights left on in rooms, hulks of cars rolled into place like props in a play . . .

The play is the tragedy Man – good old Poe,

popping up when you need him least – *it's hero,
the Conqueror Worm:*

A play. Its stage constructed by the smiling man
in the office – by the strange, ancient person
lurking behind his door.

'Cordelia!' Lander shouted. 'Cordelia! Ben!' He
waited, listening for a reply. He heard wind in the
trees, crickets and distant frogs, the sounds of
birds singing in the night as if nothing were wrong,
the laughter of a television audience.

At the end of the courtyard, a door swung open.
Ruth stepped out. 'Lander! What's wrong?'

He ran to her.

'For heaven's . . .'

He pushed her inside and shut the door.

'What is it, what's wrong?' Her frightened eyes
begged him for a quick answer. 'The kids?'

'I didn't see them. I don't know where they are,
but something's wrong here. All those cars,
they're fakes.'

'I don't . . . ' She shook her head.

'I don't know what's going on, but . . .
Remember Norman Bates?'

'Who?'

'Anthony Perkins. *Psycho*? The hotel . . .'

'Lander, stop it!'

'I don't think this is a real motel, at all. I think
it's some kind of a trap.'

'No!'

Lander leaned against the door and rubbed his
face. Always a pacifist, he'd detested firearms.
Now he wished to God he had one.

'What'll we do?' Ruth asked.

'I don't know.'

'Cordelia's out there!'

'Look, maybe I'm wrong. Maybe it's all . . . innocent, and the kids are out in the woods, or something, having the time of their lives. I don't know.'

In a quiet voice tight with control, Ruth said, 'We'd damn well better find out.'

'How?'

'We'll march ourselves right over to the office . . .'

'Oh, that's a great idea.'

'What do you suggest?'

He looked at the telephone, and immediately gave up the idea. No way to call out for help, not without going through the motel switchboard. 'We could go for help,' he muttered. 'There must be police, a sheriff . . .'

Ruth reached for the doorknob.

He grabbed her wrist.

'I'm going out there and find my daughter,' she said. 'Now let go of me.'

'Wait! We've got to think.'

'My ass! While you're thinking, God-knows-what could be happening to Cordie.' She jerked her hand free and gripped the knob. She tugged the door open.

Lander dropped backwards, slamming it shut. 'Damn it Ruth!'

'Let me out!'

The telephone rang, its harsh clamor sending a shock of alarm through Lander. Ruth's head snapped sideways. They both stood motionless, staring at the black instrument as it blared again.

Lander suddenly rushed to it. As it rang a third time, he picked it up. 'Hello?'

'Mr Dills, this is Roy in the office.'

'Yes?'

'Your daughter's here with me. She would like a word with you.'

Lander waited his eyes on Ruth.

'What is it?' she mouthed, the words barely coming out.

Lander shrugged.

'Daddy?' His daughter's voice was shrill with panic.

'Honey, what's wrong?'

'Oh Dad! They . . . Ben! I think he's dead!'

'Where are you?'

'No. Don't come. They'll kill you.'

'Are you in the office?'

'Don't let them get you!'

He motioned to Ruth. 'Here, your mother wants to talk to you.'

She hurried across the room. He handed her the phone. 'Hello, Cordie?'

'Keep her talking,' Lander whispered.

Ruth nodded.

He ran to the door, jerked it open, and rushed out. Something – a wire? – snagged his foot. As he pitched headlong, he glimpsed a grinning old woman sitting crosslegged on the hood of his car, cradling a hammer. He slammed into the dirt by the wheel.

With a squeal of delight, the woman pounced.

Chapter Five

The pickup truck lurched over a rough, dirt road. After the flare-up about Timmy, the men had kept a cold silence.

Neala wished they would talk, even fight. Their quarrel over the horny creep of a kid had pulled her mind away from thoughts of her own situation. Now, the distraction was gone. Her fear returned, black and paralyzing with images of rape and slaughter.

She began to cry. She didn't want to, didn't want the men to see her weakness, didn't want Sherri to draw more fear from her own desolation. She couldn't help it, though. She felt alone and helpless. Like the time she was lost in the woods.

She'd been only six, then, but she still remembered how it felt. Her family had been camping near Spider Lake in Wisconsin. Dad told scary stories by the campfire while they all drank hot chocolate. The hot chocolate did it: she woke in the middle of the night with a horrible strain on her bladder. She shook Betty awake, but her older sister refused to budge from the sleeping bag.

Neala had to go so badly she didn't bother to

dress. Wearing only her underpants, she crept out of the pup-tent. The chilly breeze made her shake. She crossed the campsite barefoot, the ground moist and cold under her feet.

Her dad had dug a hole, off behind the camp. A 'latrine,' he called it. Neala had been there several times, but not at night.

She wandered far into the dark woods, searching for the latrine. She couldn't find it. Finally, she gave up and squatted beside a birch tree. Relieved, she headed back for camp. She thought she knew just where it was. But she walked and walked. When she came to a strange, moonlit pasture, she knew she was lost. She called for Mom and Dad. She called for Betty. Nobody came.

That's when it hit her: the awful fear of being alone and helpless in the night. She wandered the pasture, blind with tears, wailing her anguish, hoping they would hear and come for her.

But what if someone else heard, and not her parents? One of those boogy-men Dad talked about at the campfire? Or the awful Wendigo? Or a witch like the one that tried to eat Hansel and Gretel?

Covering her mouth to stop the squalling, she ran from the pasture. In the woods, she ran as fast as she could, not daring to look back because something horrible might be chasing her. Roots tripped her. Webs stuck to her bare skin. Switches whipped her. But she kept running until she broke into another clearing and saw the moonlit car.

Their car.

They'd left it behind, and hiked a long way before making camp. She wasn't sure which way.

The doors were locked, so she crawled underneath the car. The grass beneath it was dry. She lay there, and shivered through the night, waiting.

Waiting for the boogy-man to reach under and drag her out. Waiting for the Hairy Hand to grab her, for the Wendigo to fling the car aside and sink its talons into her bare back and carry her away into the stratosphere, her feet burning to ashes with the speed of its flight.

In the morning, when Dad found her, he cried. They both cried, because everything had turned out all right, after all.

And they lived happily ever after, Neala thought, until four men and a boy put the girl into a pickup truck and drove her to a secret place in the woods, and . . .

The truck stopped.

Robbins and Shaw climbed out. 'You wait here,' Shaw told his son.

The man at Neala's feet jumped over the tailgate, and unlatched it. The gate swung down with a groan and clank. He grabbed Neala's ankles and pulled. She slid along the metal floor.

Timmy, crawling at her head, reached down suddenly and tore open her shirt. She tried to knock him away with her one free hand, but he was too quick. He squeezed her breasts as if he wanted to rip them off. Neala cried out. Her fist caught him in the face so hard it hurt her knuckles, and he fell backwards, crying.

Then she was on her feet behind the truck, Sherri at her side.

'Are you all right?' Sherri asked.

'Shut up,' Shaw said.

'Let's go,' said Robbins. His grip on Neala's arm was firm, but not painful like that of the other man.

They walked to the front of the truck. The driver had left the headlights on. The beams lit a path through a clearing, a clearing not too different from the one where Neala had wandered, lost, as a child – though that was two thousand miles away, and twenty years ago.

After a distance, the downward slanting headbeams seemed to bury themselves. The field ahead lay in darkness.

'Why the hell didn't you park closer?' Shaw whispered to the driver.

'Shut up.'

'Man, they're probably all around us.'

'They don't attack delivery parties,' said the man on Neala's right.

'Always a first time, Phillips.'

'I wouldn't sweat it.'

'I still don't see why he had to park so goddamn far away.'

'I felt like it,' the driver said. 'How about shutting your face?'

Ahead, a line of six trees stood in the clearing. Neala stared at them. They were tall and thin-trunked. Their high branches, reaching into the moonlight, were bare of leaves.

They shouldn't be bare, not in summer. They

40

should be full, their leaves fluttering in the breeze.

The trees are dead, Neala realized.

Six dead trees all in a row.

'No,' she said.

'It's all right,' Robbins whispered.

'No, don't take us there. Please.' She tried to hold back, but the men thrust her forward.

'Just take it easy,' Robbins said.

'Please! They're dead! I don't want to go there. Please!'

Pain stunned her right leg as Phillips shot a knee into it. 'Now hold it down, hon,' he said.

'You okay?' Robbins asked.

'No!'

'Christ, Phillips.'

'You've really got it bad pal. You better watch yourself.'

'Everybody shut up,' the driver snapped.

Under one of the trees they stopped.

'Lean back,' Robbins said.

'I don't . . .'

Phillips shoved Neala. Her back and head hit the trunk. Phillips held her while Shaw and the driver pushed Sherri against the same tree. She heard a rattle of handcuffs. Then the driver grabbed her right arm, pulled it backwards, and snapped the bracelet into place. Craning her neck, she saw that it was now cuffed to Sherri.

They stood back to back, hands joined, the trunk of the tree between them.

'That does it,' said the driver. He reached to his throat where something hung on a chain. He raised it to his mouth. A whistle. He blew a long, shrill note that pierced the night like the cry of a terrible bird. Then the whistle dropped from his lips. 'Let's haul ass,' he said.

Three of the men ran. The one called Robbins backed away, shaking his head. 'Sorry,' he muttered. Turning, he followed the others in their race to the pickup truck. Their sprinting forms flicked through the headlights. Then they disappeared behind the brightness. Neala heard doors bump shut, heard the tailgate bang into place. The engine rumbled to life. The headbeams swung sideways and away. For a while, the red tail lights jiggled. Then they vanished.

'Hope the fuckers rot in hell,' Sherri said.

Chapter Six

The pickup stopped in front of Robbins' house, and he jumped to the pavement.

'Have yourself a good one,' Shaw said, apparently trying to make up for his earlier behavior.

'You too,' Robbins said.

Timmy sat quietly beside his father.

'Say goodnight to Mr Robbins,' Shaw told him.

'Night,' Timmy muttered.

'Yeah.'

The truck pulled away. Robbins unlatched his front gate. He crossed the lawn toward his dark house, and sat on the porch stairs. Folding his arms over his knees, he stared at the ground.

Damn it, there was just something about that one woman – the smaller one. He'd been making delivery runs for years, ever since he turned eighteen, but he'd never felt like this before.

He'd never felt this way about any woman. Sure, there were a few he liked well enough, and some who claimed to love him. He could take his pick, whenever he got an urge to hit the sheets. But none like this.

This woman was different. Just to sit close to

her, to hold her hand, to talk with her quietly through the night . . .

By morning, she would probably be dead.

He could feel the loss, already, like a hollow in his chest.

Never to see her again.

If it were just himself, he'd go back there, maybe. He could get away, all right. They'd come for Peggy and Jenny, though.

Everybody'd have to leave. The whole family.

So why not? If they could get past the boundary, they'd be all right. He could take the woman to Los Angeles, maybe . . .

You're dreaming her life away!

Leaping to his feet, he rushed across the porch and threw open the front door. His hand hit the switch. Blinking in the sudden brightness, he crossed the room to his gun case. He took down his 30-30 Winchester, picked up a box of cartridges, and ran outside.

His old Pontiac was parked on the street. He sped two blocks to his sister's house, and ran to the screen door. He knocked hard, then entered.

'Peggy!'

She came out of the kitchen, worry on her thin face.

'For Petesakes, John . . .'

'I need to talk to you. Outside.'

Hank appeared in the kitchen doorway. He eyed Robbins with suspicion. 'What's up?' he asked.

'Nothing. Just want a word with Peg.'

Hank's eyes narrowed. 'Big secret, huh?'

'She'll tell you all about it.' Robbins grabbed his

sister's arm and pulled her out the door. He hurried across the lawn, dragging her along.

'We're getting out of here tonight,' he said.

'What?'

'Tonight's run. There was a girl. I'm going back for her.'

'Johnny, no!'

'I have to.'

'Dear God!' Oh dear God!'

'Listen, we're getting out of here. All of us.'

'No!'

'I'll get back here as soon as I can. Have Hank and Jenny ready to go.'

'Hank won't leave. You know that. He wouldn't leave here for the world.'

'That's his worry, then.'

'John, you can't do this to us!'

'Do you want to spend the rest of your life here? Do you, Peg? Do you want Jenny to grow up the way we did? Do you want her turned into a murderer like the rest of us?'

She was crying, the tears glistening in her eyes and streaming down her cheeks. 'We can't leave!'

'You *will*!'

'But Hank!'

'If he won't come along, the hell with him. You'd be better off without him anyway.'

'I suppose, but . . .'

'He can't stop you.' Johnny hugged his sister tightly. 'Don't worry, okay? We'll make it.'

She shook her head. 'Don't do this to us. Oh please, Johnny, don't!'

'Half an hour,' he said, and climbed into his car.

Chapter Seven

'We've got to get out of here,' Neala said.

'Just how do you plan to arrange it?'

'I don't *know*.' Neala's voice cracked into a sob. She turned her hands, rattling the cuffs that held her prisoner against the tree.

'We'd better think of something quick,' Sherri said. 'That whistle was some kind of a signal.'

'Maybe we can pull free.'

'Let's give it a try.'

They worked their wrists against the barkless tree behind them.

'Mine are both awfully tight,' Sherri said.

'My left seems just a bit . . .'

'Oh Jesus!' Sherri gasped, her voice dropping to a whisper.

'What's wrong?'

'Someone's in the tree.'

Neala looked to her right, tipping back her head.

'No, the other way. Beside us.'

She turned to the left. She raised her eyes up the weathered trunk to the high branches. At first, she saw only jagged limbs, pale in the moonlight like bones stripped of their flesh. Then one of them moved, and she realized it was a leg. A second leg dangled beside it. She followed them upward to a bare hip and torso, a head with shaggy hair. If there were breasts, she couldn't see them. 'Is he alive?' Neala whispered.

'I can't tell. Looks dead to me.'

Neala continued to squint upward. The figure seemed to be straddling a branch, arms at his sides. His head was tilted downward, as if he were watching her. 'I think one of the legs moved,' she said. 'Could've been the wind, I guess.'

'I hope so.'

'You hope he's dead?' Neala asked.

'Hell yes. How would you like him to come down for us?'

'God, don't say that.'

'He's probably one of *them*, whatever the fuck they are. I mean, why else would he be out here?'

Neala didn't answer. She stared at the high, motionless figure until the sound of a car engine drew her eyes away. Across the clearing, headlights appeared.

'They're coming back!'

As the headlights approached, Neala saw that they were higher than those of the pickup. 'It's someone else,' she said. 'In a van, I think.'

'Just as well,' Sherri said.

It came through the darkness, not stopping where the pickup had stopped. Its beams skittered over the ground as if seeking out Neala. They lit her and stayed, dimming just slightly when the engine shut off.

'What's going on?' Sherri asked.

'I can't see,' Neala whispered, squinting past the

headlights. 'Someone just got out. He went to the back, I think.'

'End of the line,' said a man's cheerful voice. 'All out that's getting out.'

A woman cackled.

'I think we'd better do as they say.' A man's voice. Frightened.

'Daddy!'

'Here hold onto Ben's wrist.'

'What do you want with us?' a woman demanded.

More raspy chuckles.

'I know what Rose Petal wants,' said the cheerful man. 'She wants to pound your brains out with her hammer. I'll let her, too, if you don't make it snappy.'

'Bastard.' From the girl. Then she cried out with pain.

'Damn it, leave her alone!'

'We haven't got all night.'

Several figures appeared in the darkness beyond the headlights. As they came forward, Neala saw four in a line, all cuffed together. A woman was at one side, then a man. The person at his other side was down. He and a girl each held a hand of the fallen one, dragging the limp body between them.

'Look,' said the woman.

'Hi,' Neala said.

'Step to the right,' said the cheerful man. Neala could see him, now, behind the others. He was chubby, and carried a pistol. An old, hunched woman scuttled along at his side, swinging a hammer overhead.

'Hello, young lady,' said the man with the gun. Walking around the group, he stepped up to Neala. He looked at her, grinning. With the barrel of his pistol, he pushed one side of Neala's blouse out of the way. She felt the cool muzzle stroke her nipple. 'You're a nice one. Very nice. Little Timmy got at you, I'll wager.'

'Leave me alone,' she said.

'Ah, little Timmy. Tiny Tim. He "knows where it's at," so to speak.' The man laughed, and used his hand on her other breast, cupping it, squeezing as if to test its firmness, flicking the nipple. 'Mmmm. Sometimes, I do envy those Krulls. Yes I do. Give me a little taste.' Crouching, he licked her nipple. Neala kicked. He grunted at the impact and danced away, clutching his thigh. 'Oh ho! Lucky for you, lucky for you!' He whirled toward the four chained onlookers. 'Almost got me in the 'nads!'

Neala cried out, 'No!' as he spun around, raised his pistol, and aimed toward her face. He fired. The slug smacked into the tree above her head. He lowered his aim, and fired again. The bullet ripped through the crotch of her corduroys, just missing Neala.

'Ha ha! Owed you one.' He turned away. 'Okay folks show's over. Make a circle around that tree.'

As they followed instructions, the old woman started hobbling toward Neala.

'Get away!' Neala shrieked.

Rose Petal swung the hammer as if to show off her form. Tilting her head sideways, she laughed. She limped around to the back of the tree.

'You touch me,' Sherri snapped, 'and I'll kill you.' More laughter from the old woman.

'Get away! Damn you! I'll kill you, you. . . OW! Goddamn you!'

The cuffs cut into Neala's wrist as Sherri twisted and kicked.

The old woman squealed with delight, and Neala saw her skipping sideways out of Sherri's range. Neala kicked and missed. Prancing forward, Rose Petal swung the hammer. It pounded Neala's shoulder.

A high-pitched whistle made the hag turn away.

'Let's be off, sweets,' said the chubby man.

Side by side, they hurried to the van. The doors shut. The engine turned over and the van backed up. It didn't turn around; it rolled backward across the clearing and disappeared into the woods.

'Now what?' asked the girl beneath the other tree. All four were in a circle around it, hands joined as if playing 'Ring Around the Rosie.'

'Young ladies,' the man called. 'Do you know what's going on?'

Neala shook her head.

'They just – kidnapped us!' he said. 'Right out of the motel.'

'We were at the coffee shop,' Sherri told him.

'Do you know why they brought us here?' asked the woman.

'For the Krulls,' Sherri said.

'The what?'

'Krulls. I don't know. Krulls? We're sacrifices or something.'

'That's crazy,' the man said.

'Don't I know it,' Sherri muttered.

'It's crazy,' the man repeated.

'You're damn right,' Sherri said. 'Look, we've gotta get out of here. These things are gonna come for us. One's already here.' She pointed at the tree high above the four strangers.

Neala looked, along with the others, and saw the pale figure suddenly swing downward, dropping from branch to branch.

'Oh my God!'

Screams and shouts of panic erupted from those beneath the tree as it scurried down the trunk. They threw themselves outward, trying to get away, and yelled in pain as the cuffs tore into their wrists. The unconscious one, arms jerked by those at his sides, raised his head. The others didn't seem to notice. They leaped and squirmed as the naked man dropped into their circle.

He pounced on the woman's back, his weight knocking her forward until the ring of arms stopped her. She recoiled backward. The whole circle fell.

The strange, bony man was pinned beneath her. Neala saw his legs wrap the woman's hips. His hands appeared beneath her outstretched arms and wildly tore her blouse as she thrashed above him. He jerked the blouse off her shoulders. His mouth clamped down on her left shoulder, and she screamed.

Then he was writhing out from under her. He crawled to her kicking feet. Kneeling over her, he grabbed one.

'Hey!'

He raised his head, mouth gaping, and looked toward the woods behind him.

Neala looked, too.

A man was running toward them.

The naked man stood. His shaggy head jerked from side to side, as if he hoped to find help. Then, with a bellow that made Neala's skin shrivel, he raced toward the intruder.

The other man stopped. He raised a rifle. Its detonation slammed through the night and the naked man pitched forward.

Chapter Eight

Robbins sprinted past the body. Ignoring the shouts from the group of four, he headed toward the tree with the two women. He slung the rifle over his shoulder and dug a hand into his pocket. He pulled out a key.

'We're getting out of here.'

The woman he wanted stared at him, looking confused.

He stepped to her right side, and unlocked the cuff.

'You're one of the men from the truck,' she said.

'That's right. I'm taking you out of here. I've got a car off in the trees.' He stepped past her, and started unlocking the cuff on her other wrist. 'Are you a good runner?' he asked.

She shrugged.

'What's your name?'

'Neala.'

I'm Johnny Robbins.'

'I'm Sherri,' said the bigger woman, appearing from behind the tree. She held out her hands, empty bracelets dangling from the wrists. 'Do me a favor, huh?'

Quickly, he removed the cuffs. Unslinging his

rifle, he scanned the perimeters of the clearing. Over the shouts of the other captives, he could hear the howling of distant Krulls. No sign of them, though.

'Okay,' he said. 'This way.'

'Wait,' Neala said. 'We can't leave *them*.' She nodded toward the others.

'The hell we can't. Let's go.' He grabbed Neala's arm, but she jerked free.

'I'm not going without them.'

'Shit,' her friend said.

Neala whirled on her. 'What's the matter with you? How can you even *think* of leaving these people?'

'To save my sweet ass, for Godsake.'

'We can't!'

Robbins groaned. It was stupid to waste time freeing the others. The delay could be fatal. But if he didn't give it a shot, he wouldn't stand much of a chance with Neala. 'All right,' he said. 'Stick close.'

They followed him to the other tree.

'Everybody shut up!' he snapped at the four.

They went silent. He stepped in front of the older male.

'You'll have to take care of the others,' he said, unlocking the right wrist. 'I'll leave you the key. We're going on ahead. If I can, I'll hold the car for you.' The other cuff fell loose. He slapped the key into the man's palm. 'Good luck.' He turned to Neala. 'Okay?'

'Okay.'

'Let's haul it.'

They started to run. Robbins took the lead, holding back to stay with the women. They were much slower than he'd hoped. Damn it, he should have parked the car closer. He'd left it much too far away, wanting to come in silently on foot. Sneak in, sneak out. With luck, he might have taken Neala out quickly, without a sound, and been on the road before anyone knew. If he hadn't shot that one bastard . . .

They were almost to the edge of the clearing when Neala grabbed his arm. 'Wait,' she gasped. 'We've got to wait.'

'What?'

She pointed to the group that was still at the distant row of trees, the man busy unlocking cuffs. 'Forget 'em,' Robbins snapped.

'How'll they find the car?'

'Doesn't matter. Come on.'

'Christ, Neala!' Sherri snarled.

'Look!' Robbins pointed at a far-off figure loping across the field toward the group. 'There's another. Another.' Scanning the clearing, he could make out half a dozen dark shapes: some running, others limping, another scurrying across the ground like a crab.

'Oh my God!' Neala gasped.

'In a few more minutes, there'll be dozens. They'll get us, too, if we stick around much longer.' He pulled Neala into the woods. She tried to struggle free, at first. Then she was running close behind him. He dashed between the dark posts of tree trunks, kicked his way through waist-high bushes, dodged thickets too dense to penetrate, leapt onto the back of a fallen tree and jumped down to its other side.

Pausing while the women caught up, he listened.

The howling had stopped, but he heard Krulls nearby: feet crushing foliage, wheezing breath, the gibber of their strange language.

'Almost there,' he whispered.

'They're everywhere,' Sherri muttered. 'We'll never make it.'

'We'll make it.'

They kept running. Finally, they reached the roadhead where Robbins had left his car. He scanned the area. 'We're all right,' he said. 'Come on.'

Crouching low, he ran to the car. The women stayed close behind him. He grabbed the nearest handle. He was about to tug the door open, but a movement caught his eye. He looked up.

The face in the car window twisted, showing teeth.

Neala yelped with fright.

Robbins stared at the face. It was badly scarred.

The nose was a ragged flap, as if it had been chewed off in a fight.

There were five other faces inside the car, all turned his way.

Something clutched his foot. He lurched backwards, knocking into the girls, kicking the hand that had him by the ankle. Three Krulls started squirming out from under the car.

The doors opened.

Robbins rammed his rifle to his shoulder, took quick aim at the noseless face, and fired. The top of the head flew off.

'Let's go!' he yelled.

'Where?'

He fired again; this time taking out the eye of one by the rear door.

'Run! For Christsake, run!'

Free of the cuffs, they ran. Lander led the way, taking them across the clearing toward the place where the other three had vanished into the timber.

He took them that way in spite of the gunshots, in spite of the woman moving toward them from that direction. She was alone, a stooped old crone with white hair and pendulous breasts flapping down to her waist. She was armed with a machete, but her crippled back prevented her from moving fast. Lander simply planned to run around her.

'Dad!'

With a quick glance around, he saw a man on the heels of Cordelia. Two more were close behind. Ben dropped back and threw a shoulder block into the nearest one. They both tumbled sideways.

Looking ahead, Lander saw the old woman hobbling toward him. He lunged sideways as the machete slashed. He heard it cut through the air, saw it flash past his cheek, felt the breath of its close passage. He tripped and fell. The crone came after him, swinging. She stood over him. Raised the machete.

Whimpering, Lander shut his eyes tightly.

The blade didn't fall.

'Lander!' He looked. Ruth was behind the old woman, clutching the upraised arm, dragging her backwards.

He clambered to his feet. He drove a knee into the sagging belly. Foul breath blew into his face. Reaching up with both hands; he twisted the machete loose.

He hacked sideways, careful to miss Ruth's arm across the hag's throat. The blade slashed into one of the hanging breasts. Horrified, he watched the pale sack of flesh fall away.

Ruth let go as the woman dropped to her knees, screaming. Lander swung the machete straight down. It missed the center of the head, glanced off, took away half the scalp, and chopped into the shoulder. He tried again, this time splitting the head.

With a quick jerk, he pulled the blade free. He ran to where Ben and Cordelia were struggling with three men. One had Cordelia around the waist, trying to lift her. She kicked backward and squirmed. Lander circled, but the man turned, too, keeping Cordelia in the way. Finally, Lander threw himself against his daughter. The man stumbled and fell. As he hit the ground, Cordelia twisted free and Lander swung. The blade bit into an upthrust arm. The man bellowed with pain. He rolled out of the way, and Lander's next blow missed. Then he was on his feet and running.

Lander turned to Ben. The boy sat astraddle one, punching down at the face. A second man was behind Ben, about to bash him with a club. Lander's machete caught the standing one in the spine. With a cry, the man jerked stiff and dropped his club. A white club. A bone with a ball-joint at one end.

'Dad!' Cordelia called.

He tried to pull the machete free. It was stuck in the man's back.

'Dad, My God!'

Ruth was already far away, forty or fifty yards away, almost to the edge of the forest – slung over the shoulder of a tall, pale figure.

Lander whirled around. 'Ben, get off!'

Ben rolled away. The half-conscious man raised his head. Lander kicked it hard, and the man went limp.

He turned in time to see Ruth disappear into the woods.

'Stay close to me!' he yelled, and began the chase.

Just to the right, three people ran out from among the trees.

'Over there!' Lander called to them. 'Over there! He's got my wife!' The two groups met, and entered the timber.

Chapter Nine

Peg quietly pushed open the door, half expecting to find Jenny asleep. Instead, the girl was propped up with pillows, reading a mystery. Her bare feet were crossed at the ankles. Peg realized, vaguely, that her daughter had nearly outgrown the pink pajamas, that Christmas would be too long to wait . . .

'What's up?' Jenny asked.

Peg shut the door. 'I want you to get dressed.'

'Now?'

'Right now.'

The girl wrinkled her nose. 'I don't get it.'

'We're going on a trip.'

'We *are*?' Her delight only lasted an instant. Then she frowned. 'Where are we going?'

'Away with Uncle John. Now hurry up and get dressed. Jeans and a blouse are fine.'

Jenny's eyes widened. She pressed the open book to her belly, and leaned forward. In a voice hushed and eager with conspiracy she said, 'It's Hank. We're running away from Hank!'

'We're not running away. We're just going on a vacation.'

'Don't worry, I won't tell.' Jenny swung herself

off the bed. 'Where're we going? How about Los Angeles?' She flung her pajama shirt aside as she headed for the closet. 'Wouldn't you just love to go to Disneyland? We can go there, can't we?'

'Sure,' Peg said.

'Which blouse should I wear?'

'The plaid's fine.'

Jenny pulled the plaid blouse off its hanger. She slid her arms inside as she hurried toward the dresser. The sight of her small, pointed breasts reminded Peg that they'd planned to go shopping, this week, for a bra. Jenny's first. Now, that would have to wait.

Like everything else.

With John's visit, their normal world had come to an unexpected, abrupt halt. Nothing would ever be the same.

It hadn't been such a great life, up to now. She'd often dreamed of changing it, of leaving Hank, of taking Jenny far away. Now, she only wished that it could go on in the same old way.

It couldn't. John had dropped the bomb.

Trembling, she sat on the corner of Jenny's bed.

'Are you sick or something?' Jenny asked.

'I'm okay.'

'You look like you're gonna die.'

A chill crawled up Peg's back. 'Don't say that.'

'We've got to make sure and go to the Haunted House.'

'Huh?'

'And Space Mountain.' She kicked off her pajama bottoms, and stepped into her cotton underpants. 'Uncle John'll take me, if you don't

64

want to. I'll be the only one in class who's been on Space Mountain. Harriet Hayer went to Disneyland, but her dad wouldn't let her. He's a creep, even if he is the mayor.'

Jenny fastened her jeans, and sat on the bed to pull on her socks. Peg put an arm around her.

'What happens if Hank catches us?'

'He won't.'

'Where is he?'

'Watching TV'

'Want me to climb out the window? We can both climb out. Is Uncle John coming in his car?'

'Yes.'

'When?'

'Any minute.'

'We ought to fix Hank's car. I could give it a flat tire. You want me to? Then he can't chase us.'

'No, you don't have to.'

'It'd be easy.'

'It's all right.'

Jenny finished tying her sneakers, and turned to Peg. 'We're never going to come back ever, are we?'

Peg shook her head.

'I didn't think so.' She shrugged her small shoulders. 'Oh well.'

'What?'

'Nothing. It's just that . . . well, Robbie Taylor, he was going to take me bowling tomorrow. I guess I won't ever see him again, huh?'

Peg brushed her fingers through Jenny's soft, brown hair.

'Or Marilou, either.' Her lips began to tremble,

and tears filled her eyes. She looked at Peg, blinking, as if waiting for an answer that would make everything all right again.

Peg had no answer for her. 'Come on,' she said, and led the girl to the window. Silently, she slid the window up. The screen remained, its frame hooked into place at the bottom. She flicked open the hooks, and pushed. The snug frame didn't budge.

'You have to whack it,' Jenny told her.

'If we make any noise . . .'

'I'll do it.' Jenny wiped the tears off her face. Then she went to her bed for the book. Holding its upper edge against the frame, she struck the bottom sharply with her palm. The screen popped outward. 'Now it just slides out,' she said.

'Can you do it?'

'Sure.'

Peg held her by the hips while Jenny gripped the sides of the screen, and pulled.

'It's stuck.'

'For Godsake, don't drop it!'

'I . . .'

It suddenly fell free. Jenny gasped. The screen crashed into the bushes below the window and banged into the wall. 'Oh no,' she muttered. She turned to Peg, shaking her head. 'I'm sorry, Mom. I didn't mean to, honest. It just slipped.'

'It's all right, honey.'

'Maybe he didn't hear it.'

'Maybe not.'

Jenny leaned out the window.

'Bitch!'

Hank, just outside, grabbed the front of her blouse and jerked her through the window. Peg reached for the girl's feet. Too late. Hank flung her to the ground.

'You bastard!' Peg cried.

Hank grinned up at her. Then he turned away. Crouching over Jenny, he grabbed her by the collar and belt.

'Leave her alone!'

'Try and stop me.'

He raised the struggling girl waist-high, and dropped her.

'No!' Peg shrieked. She threw a leg over the window sill and started to climb out. Hank clutched her arm. He tugged. He wrenched the arm as if trying to drive her head into the ground, but her shoulder hit first. He shoved her onto her back, and sat on her. Pinning her hands to the ground, he bounced on her belly.

'Okay,' he said. He was breathless above her, and sweating. 'Okay, what's going on. Huh? What're you trying to pull?'

'Nothing.'

'Nothing? You and the kid were running off!'

'No.'

'You want me to hurt the kid?'

'Hank, for Godsake!'

'Set her hair on fire?'

'You bastard!'

'Where were you going? To Phillips?'

'No.'

'That shithead has always been after your ass.'

'It wasn't him!'

'Then who?'

'Nobody.'

'Okay, the kid gets it.'

As he scurried off Peg, she grabbed his foot. He kicked free and rushed to Jenny. The girl was still face down. He grabbed a handful of hair and lifted it from her back. His other hand snatched a butane lighter from his shirt pocket.

'No!' Peg yelled. 'I'll tell, I'll tell!'

She crawled toward him.

Hank thumbed the lighter. A flame spurted high.

'It was John! He's coming for us! He went out to the Killing Trees for a woman, and he's going to take us away!'

Hank grinned. 'Oh yeah? Not anymore, he's not.'

Chapter Ten

Neala's feet throbbed with pain. Dozens of times, she cursed that little prick, Timmy, for taking her shoes. The pain and anger helped her hold onto reality as she followed the man named Robbins to his car, found it full of Krulls like a strange family about to embark on a vacation, watched him shoot two of them dead, and ran for her life away from the car.

Finding the other group again had been a relief, at first. Strength in numbers. But the man, Lander, didn't care about staying quiet or hiding. He wanted only to find his wife, even if it got the rest of them killed.

'We'll never find her,' Robbins said after ten minutes of wandering through the dense trees. 'We'd better give it up and try to make our way to the main road.'

'Go ahead,' Lander snapped. 'Who needs you?'

'You'll get your kids killed.'

'I've got to find my wife.'

'She's probably dead already.'

'No.'

'How can we possibly find her?' asked the girl.

She sounded desperate, on the edge of tears.

'We can't if we don't try,' Lander said. 'We can't if we do nothing but cower in the bushes like whipped curs.'

'It's our only chance,' Robbins said.

' "A coward dies many times. A brave man never tastes of death but once." '

'I'm with Mr Dills,' said the boy. 'We've got to save her, even if it means taking some extra chances.'

'Fuck it,' Sherri said. 'I'm not gonna risk my ass . . .'

Lander yelped as a pale figure dropped out of a tree. The knees rammed his shoulders, driving him down. Neala saw a knife in the upraised hand. Robbins fired. A hole appeared between the small breasts. The girl tumbled forward and hit the ground face first.

'Holy fucking shit!' Sherri gasped.

Neala stared down at the body. The girl was naked. Blood gushed from the ragged hole in her back.

'Let's go,' Robbins snapped. 'The shot'll bring 'em running.'

He pulled Neala by the hand.

They ran. They ran for a long distance. Neala's feet throbbed with pain as she kept pace with Robbins, but she didn't complain or slow down. For the first time since her capture at the diner, she felt hopeful. She was no longer anyone's prisoner, Robbins seemed determined to save her, and the Krulls had dropped out of sight. Maybe she would survive the night, after all.

Finally, when she thought she could run no farther, Robbins stopped.

'We'll just . . . catch our breath,' he gasped.

Neala nodded.

Sherri, who'd been running a short distance behind her, caught up. She sagged against a tree trunk.

'Where're the others?' Robbins asked.

'Coming.' Sherri flopped an arm sideways. 'Back there someplace. Christ on a crutch, I can hardly move.'

Neala heard the crunch of rushing feet. Off to the left. She raised her voice to call out. 'Ov . . .' Robbins clapped a hand across her mouth.

'Shhhh.'

His hand had a pungent odor like gunsmoke.

'Might not be them,' he whispered.

'Hey!' called a voice. The boy's voice. 'Where'd you all go?'

Robbins nodded and dropped his hand.

'Over here,' Neala called.

A few moments later, the boy and girl joined them.

'Sorry,' gasped the boy. 'Got a little lost.'

'Dad?' The girl staggered as if lost in a dark room. 'Dad? Where are you?' She looked at Robbins. 'Where's my dad?'

'I haven't seen him.'

She turned to the boy. 'Oh God, Ben, what'll we do?'

'He'll show up. We'll just wait.'

'Five minutes,' Robbins said. 'Who's got a watch?'

71

The girl raised her hand, and Neala saw a band on her wrist. For a moment, she was puzzled that the watch hadn't been stolen, back in town. Then she thought about Rose Petal. No surprise, really, that the old bag didn't care about such loot. Too far gone for that. Her big thrill was bouncing her hammer off skulls. And that guy, the sadistic . . .

'What's the time?' Robbins asked.

The girl pressed a button. Red numbers glowed at her wrist. 'Ten thirty-two.'

'We'll give him till ten forty'

'Then what?' the girl asked.

'Then we move fast.'

'Maybe *you* do.'

'We're giving him eight minutes.' Robbins' voice was a quiet, calm whisper. 'If he hasn't shown up by then, he probably won't show at all. He either got lost, or the Krulls nailed him. Either way, we could stick around here till we've got Krulls crawling up our . . . till they get us, and it won't do your father any good.'

'Well, I'm not leaving.'

'That's up to you.'

'Maybe he'll get here in time,' the boy said.

The talking stopped. They waited.

Neala looked into the trees. Except for a few shreds of moonlight, the woods were as dark as a shut closet. The father was out there, someplace. But she didn't expect him to show up. If anyone came out of there, it wouldn't be him.

She rubbed her arms. She turned, staring into the darkness.

If anyone came out . . .

She stepped close to a tree, and leaned back against it. The bark felt rough through her shirt. It felt good.

At least they can't come up behind me, she thought.

Robbins asked the time.

'Ten thirty-five,' whispered the girl.

Only *three* minutes had passed.

Neala moaned. She crossed her arms. Her nipples were erect and aching, as if she had a chill. She covered them with her hands, and the comforting warm pressure eased the tightness.

Off to the right, a twig popped.

Neala looked in that direction. She saw only trees and bushes and darkness. Nothing moved. No more sounds came.

But she kept her eyes on that patch of darkness. She barely breathed.

Because someone was out there watching.

She could feel him. She could almost see him, but not quite.

Someone.

Someone not the girl's father.

Chapter Eleven

'Just sit there,' Hank ordered.

Peg lowered herself again to the sofa, where Hank had shoved her after dragging her inside the house.

He stood across the room, holding Jenny by the hair. Jenny, on her knees, kept sobbing. 'Don't move an inch,' he warned her. Then he let go of her hair, and dialed the phone. When he finished dialing, he gripped it again.

'Yes. This is Hank Stover. I've got a situation here. Is Chief Murdoch around? . . . No? Well, send out one of the boys, would you? . . . No, nothing like that. I've got matters well in hand.' He grinned at his joke, and wrenched Jenny's hair. 'That's 833 Nussbaum Road . . . Right. I appreciate it.'

He hung up, and pulled Jenny to her feet. 'Okay, go sit with your mother.'

She sat beside Peg and leaned against her, crying softly. Peg put her arm around the girl.

'You did it this time,' Hank said. 'You and your damn brother. You're gonna get us *all* killed, you know that?' Shaking his head, he leaned back against the wall and folded his arms. 'That guy's really done it. Christ, you don't monkey with the Krulls. They're gonna come for us, you know that, don't you?'

'That's why we have to leave.'

'Yeah. Leave, my ass. What we'll do, we'll grab your hotshot brother when he shows up. That's what we'll do. We'll take him to the Trees. Maybe that'll be enough. Some brother you got. Flushes us all down the shitter for a piece of tail.'

'Don't you *want* to get out of here?'

'I like it here fine, thanks. I've got a good business . . .'

'Sure. Selling dead people's cars.'

He jabbed a finger at her. 'Not in front of the kid, damn it!'

'You think she doesn't know? She knows. Tell him,' Peg said to the girl.

Jenny shook her head.

'Tell him!' she snapped.

'I know!' Jenny blurted.

'Know what?' Hank asked.

'You get the cars . . . from the people we give to the Krulls.'

'Who told you that?'

'Everyone knows.'

He lunged toward her and raised a fist. Jenny covered her face. 'Lois Murdoch!' she yelled.

'Charlie's kid?'

'Yes. She said you get to keep part of the money, and her dad gets part, and part goes to the town.'

'It's no big secret,' Peg added.

'Hey, that's perfectly all right by me. They all

76

get their share. It's not like I'm the only one taking advantage of the situation.'

'You more than most.'

'Yeah? Well I didn't see you complaining when you got the dishwasher. Or the TV for the bedroom. Or the . . .'

'You could've got a clean job.'

'Sure. Like your sainted brother, the grease monkey?'

'He's a fine mechanic. His money hasn't got blood on it.'

'Ah. He's pure as the falling snow. Except he's been a Delivery Man since he was eighteen.' Hank smirked. 'He's a *real* sweet guy.'

'He didn't have a choice.'

'Sure. They held a gun to his head. Don't give me that. Know why he's a Delivery Man? 'Cause he likes it. He gets off on the power.'

'You don't know what you're talking about.'

'Don't I? There's nothing he likes better than getting his paws on those . . .'

The doorbell rang.

'Don't move,' he warned. He went to the door and opened it. 'Come on in.'

Looking over her shoulder, Peg saw Dave Fielding enter. At twenty-three, he was the youngest man in the Barlow Police Department. He fidgeted, and smiled uneasily at Peg and Jenny.

'What seems to be the trouble, Mr Stover?'

'John Robbins.'

'I see.' He had trouble unbuttoning his shirt pocket. He pulled out a note pad, and a Bic pen. He wrote on the pad as Hank continued.

'Robbins is my wife's brother. What happened, I caught her trying to sneak out tonight with her daughter.'

'*Her* daughter?'

'By a previous marriage.'

'Her father,' Peg said, 'is . . . he disappeared.'

'I see.' Fielding glanced at Hank. 'So you're the girl's stepfather.'

'Right. Now I caught the two of them trying to sneak out. It seems that Robbins went back to the Trees, tonight . . .'

'He's a Delivery Man, isn't he?'

'Right. He apparently got the hots for a gal, tonight, and went back to the trees to rescue her.'

'*Jesus*,' Fielding muttered. He glanced at Peg, and blushed.

'After he gets the gal, he's planning to come back for Peg and the kid, and they're all gonna make a break for it.'

'Wow.'

'What I think we should do is grab him when he shows up . . .'

'And take him out to the Trees,' Fielding finished.

'Right.'

'When do you expect him?'

'Any time, now. It's been about an hour.'

'You realize, he probably won't show up.'

'Knowing Robbins, he might pull it off.'

Fielding shook his head and slipped the pad into his uniform pocket. 'If he does come, we'll need some back-up.'

'You'd better get your car out of sight, too.'

'That goes without saying. Now, may I use your phone?'

'Right over there.'

Fielding stepped over to the telephone, and dialed.

Jenny leaned close to Peg's ear. 'I've got to *go*,' she whispered.

'Can't you hold it?'

'No.'

'Hank, Jenny has to use the bathroom.'

'Wait'll the cop's done.'

'Fielding,' he said into the phone. I need a back-up team over at the Stover place.' He checked his note pad '833 Nussbaum . . . Marks and Haycraft are fine. Tell 'em to hurry.' He hung up.

'Now can I go?' Jenny asked.

'You want to watch my wife?' Hank asked Fielding. 'I'll take the kid to the john.'

'I don't want *you* to come!'

'Tough tittie. I'm not gonna have you sneaking out.'

'No! You'll watch!'

She turned to Fielding. 'He's a pervert! He's always spying on me.'

Hank's face turned purple. 'You lying little bitch, what're you trying to pull?'

'It's just 'cause it's the truth!'

Hank's fists clenched, but he stayed back. He looked at Fielding. 'You know why she's doing this? She wants you to take her to the john. I don't know what she's got up her sleeve, but she's a clever kid. She's always reading books, you know? Mysteries and stuff. Thinks she's Nancy Drew.'

'You want me to take her?' Fielding asked. His face was red.

'Help yourself. But watch out.'

Fielding gestured to the girl. 'Come on, then.'

She gave Hank a smug glance, and hurried to Fielding's side.

'There's a window,' Hank warned. 'Don't let her shut the door.'

Jenny took hold of Fielding's hand, and led him away. Hank shook his head. He turned to Peg. 'She's gonna pull something, just wait and see.'

Fielding entered the bathroom and went to the window on its far wall. It was plenty big enough for the girl to climb out, but the screen was firmly in place. He shut the window and latched it.

'All right,' he said.

'Can I shut the door?' she asked.

'Okay. But I'll only give you half a minute. Then I'm coming in, whether you're ready or not.'

'What if I lock the door?' She grinned up at him.

'I'd have to break it down.'

'That'd be neat.'

'I'd rather not have to.'

'Okay.' She shut the door.

Fielding listened for the click of the lock, but it didn't come. He raised his left arm. The second-hand of his wristwatch moved slowly past the numbers. After thirty seconds, he knocked lightly. 'Time's up.'

'I'm almost done.'

'Hurry it up.'

The toilet flushed. He heard water run for a

moment. Then the door opened. She smiled up at him.

'Hank really would've watched, you know. He's sick in the head.'

'Come on, let's get going.'

'Can I tell you a secret?' She wiggled a finger, and glanced nervously down the hallway. 'I've gotta whisper.'

Fielding shrugged, and crouched down. Her lips tickled his ear. 'You know what Hank does to me?' she whispered. 'Late at night, he comes sneaking into my bedroom, sometimes, and he . . .'

The girl's hand moved swiftly. Fielding felt a strange, hot line across his throat. For an instant, he thought she'd scratched him with a fingernail. Then blood sprayed her face. His blood. He shoved her away. He tried to stand. Dizzy, he lurched toward the wall. The spray of blood moved as he did, and painted the wall.

He staggered back. He reached for his revolver, but his hand seemed too clumsy to unsnap the leather guard. Then he was staring at the ceiling. Blood showered down, filling his eyes, and he didn't have the strength to wipe it away.

Jenny slipped the injector blade into the pocket of her blouse and dropped to her knees beside the policeman. She popped open a snap that held his revolver inside its holster. She pulled the revolver out.

Standing, she looked down at the man. Blood still ran from his slit throat, but it no longer gushed.

She felt sick.

He'd seemed like a nice man.

But he would have helped kill Uncle John. He had to be stopped. It was the right thing to do. The right thing.

She suddenly doubled over and vomited. The spasms tore at her insides. Her eyes filled with tears.

I've got to stop!

I've got to . . .

Another contraction hit, sending a gush through her mouth and nostrils. A motion down the hallway caught her eyes. Blinking tears away, she looked up.

Hank ran toward her.

With both hands, she raised the revolver.

'No!' He stopped. 'Don't shoot! You did right! Now we can make our getaway.'

The first bullet knocked a leg out from under him. Jenny watched him flop. He lay on his belly, raising himself with his arms.

'Jenny, please!'

She took careful aim at his face, and pulled the trigger five times very quickly, staring through the white smoke as pieces of his head exploded away and hit the walls.

Chapter Twelve

The roar of gunshots pounded through Peg's head. She raised her face off the carpet and looked toward the hallway.

Jenny!

Jenny's down there!

She pushed herself to her hands and knees. Grabbing the edge of the coffee table, she struggled to her feet. She straightened up. She wobbled a bit, still dizzy from the blow to her temple. Hank, hearing the commotion in the hall, had slammed her with a beer bottle to keep her from running. She stepped over the still unbroken bottle, and staggered toward the hallway.

A tattered layer of smoke hung over the bodies, swirling in the air currents as Jenny rushed from Hank's body to Fielding's. Peg glanced down at the body of her husband. His head . . . she quickly looked away, and saw the tiny, bright blade in his outstretched hand.

'Come here,' Jenny said. 'But don't step in the blood.'

'Jenny?'

'We've gotta get out of here,' the girl said. She

wrapped Fielding's fingers around the revolver grips.

Peg watched, stunned and confused. Jenny was sheathed with blood, her hair matted with it, her shirt splattered. 'Are . . . are you hurt?'

The girl smirked. 'They didn't touch me. I blew it, though. Boy, did I blow it. If I'd kept out of the blood, we could've stuck around and played innocent.'

'What are . . . ?'

'We've got to split. Come on. The back door.'

Peg followed her daughter into the kitchen. The girl hurried to the sink, turned on the water, and rinsed her hands.

'Shouldn't we hurry?' Peg asked.

'I figure they won't get here in under five minutes, so we've got a couple left.' She dried her hands on a paper towel and stuffed the wadded towel into her pocket.

Amazed, Peg watched Jenny step over to the silverware drawer and pull it open as casually as if she were preparing to set the dinner table. Her hand came out with four steak knives.

'What are those for?'

'In case . . .'

The doorbell rang, knotting Peg's stomach with fear. Jenny rushed to the kitchen door, opened it silently, and pointed out.

They raced through the yard to the tool shed in the rear, and ran behind it. Jenny stopped. She leaned back against the wall.

'Where'll we go?' Peg asked. For a moment, she thought how strange it was to be relying on her twelve-year-old daughter. But the girl seemed to know what she was doing. She'd always had a lot of common sense and nerve – too much nerve, Peg often thought.

'To Phillips?' Jenny asked.

Peg stared at her. 'What do you mean?'

'Hank said . . .'

'I know what he said, and it's not true.'

'Come *on*, Mom. I'm not a baby. I know you've been going with someone.'

'That's enough!'

'If it's not Phillips, who is it?'

'None of your business young lady.'

'Look, we need help. We can't just wander around the streets, for gosh sakes. We need a hideout or a car, one or the other. Do you know how to hot-wire a car?'

'Of course not.'

'Me neither. They do it in books all the time, but I can't. I tried on Hank's car a couple times, but – I don't know – there's more to it than meets the eye. I think we'd better try Phillips.'

'What about John? He'll come by, and . . .'

'And see the cop cars, and keep going. Here, take these.' Jenny gave her two of the steak knives. 'Hide them.' She watched Jenny lift a cuff of her jeans and slip a knife into her sock. The other went into her hip pocket, handle first.

Peg was wearing a sleeveless, belted dress. Her feet were bare in her sandals. She shook her head. 'Where?'

'Have you got panties on?'

'Of course.'

85

Jenny patted her hips. 'Put them at the sides.'

Peg lifted her dress and slipped a knife under each side of her panties. The blades were cool on her skin. She adjusted the knives until she could no longer feel their sharp, serrated edges. 'Okay,' she said.

'Now let's go to Phillips.'

'Jenny!'

'Mom, they'll take us to the Killing Trees.'

'But . . .'

'Do you want the Krulls to get us? My gosh, you *know* what they'll do!'

'Just rumors,' she mumbled.

'Well, I believe them, don't you? If Phillips loves you, he'll help us. Now come on!'

Jenny pushed away from the wall and hurried to the gate. She unlatched it and opened it an inch. She peered through the gap, opened the gate wider, and stuck her head out. After looking both ways, she glanced back at Peg. 'The alley's clear,' she whispered.

Peg followed her through the gate. They rushed across the dark alley and ducked beside a telephone pole. 'Where's his house?' Jenny asked.

'Third and Division.'

'Geez, that's the other side of town.'

'I know that.'

'We can't make it that far, not even cutting through yards. They'd be sure to . . . I've *got* it!'

'What?'

'Tucker Grady. He's on vacation. I saw him drive off in his jeep yesterday. He's a bachelor. His house'll be deserted.'

'So?'

'It's deserted. We can use it.'

'You mean, break in?'

'Sure. Why not?'

'It's against the . . . ' The look on Jenny's face stopped her. Against the law. A hell of a thing to worry about at a time like this. 'Do you think we can get in?' she asked.

'No sweat. Come on.'

They made their way cautiously down the alley, staying close to the left side. They were nearly to the end of the block when a car turned in. Jenny pulled Peg down. They ducked behind a pair of garbage cans. The car moved slowly toward them.

'Bet it's a cop car,' Jenny whispered.

'Do you think they saw us?'

'It would've sped up.'

Peg hunched lower as the car approached. She heard its radio crackle and sputter, heard the loud, staccato voice of the dispatcher blasting unintelligible phrases. The wheels crunched over the crumbling macadam less then a yard away. She caught a whiff of cigar smoke. The car kept moving. The sweet cigar odor faded along with the sounds of the radio.

'Don't move till they're out of the alley,' Jenny warned. 'The rear-view mirror.'

When the sounds of the car were gone, Jenny stood. She leaned over the top of her trash can and peered down the alley. 'It's okay,' she whispered.

They ran the rest of the way. Tucker Grady's house was second from the last. The yard wasn't fenced. A thick hedge of bushes shielded it from the alley. Near Grady's trash cans, Jenny found a space through the bushes.

They entered the back yard. The rear windows of the small, single-story house were dark.

'Are you sure it's empty?' Peg asked.

'It better be.'

Staying low, they rushed through the yard. Jenny crept up the steps to the screened-in porch. She took the knife from her back pocket, slit the screen, and reached in to unlock the door. They entered the porch.

Peg stood just inside the screen door, holding it open, ready to dash out if the door of the house should suddenly burst open. She held her breath as Jenny tried the knob.

'Locked.'

The girl stepped back, and looked along the wall of the house. 'Ah-ha,' she said. She climbed onto an old couch against the wall, stood on its back, and tried to force open a small, high window. It didn't budge. Jumping to the floor, she glanced around. She stepped over to a bumper pool table in the corner. Two cue sticks lay across its top. She picked up one, and returned to the couch. Standing on its cushion, she thumped the cue's heavy end against the glass as if taking aim, then drew back and shot it forward, smashing a hole through the window.

Peg cringed at the sudden noise. Her eyes darted to the door.

Jenny, standing on the couch, also watched the door. She held the cue stick overhead like a club, ready to bash anyone who might come out.

The door stayed shut.

Jenny set the cue aside. Climbing onto the back of the couch, she reached through the broken window and unlocked it. She slid the window up.

'I'll go through,' she whispered, 'and open the door for you.'

'Don't cut yourself, honey. Do you want a boost?'

'Nah,' Jenny said, and climbed head first through the window. In moments, she was gone.

Peg waited in the dark porch. She looked at the open window and wished she had gone into the house instead of Jenny. She should have been the one. It wasn't right, letting Jenny take such risks. If harm came to her . . .

What was taking her so long?

Peg stepped toward the window. It looked high and small. Jenny had climbed through it easily, but it wouldn't be so simple for Peg.

She decided to give her daughter another minute. Slowly, she began counting to sixty.

One, two three, four . . . She heard footsteps inside. Five, six . . . The lock clacked and the door swung open. Jenny smiled out at her.

'What took you so long?' Peg whispered.

'I hurried as fast as I could.'

'It's okay. I was just worried.' She entered the kitchen, and shut the door.

'There's only one thing,' Jenny said.

'What?'

'Someone's in the bedroom.'

'Oh God!'

'It's just some old lady. Besides, she's asleep.'

'Let's get out of here!'

'No, it's all right.'

'What if she wakes up?'

'There's two of us, and only one of her. Besides she's ancient. And . . . ' Jenny opened a lower button of her blouse and reached inside. 'I got these. They were next to her bed.'

Peg stared through the darkness. 'Glasses?'

'Yeah. And a hearing aid. Without these, she's useless.' Jenny set them on the kitchen table beside a ring of keys. She nodded toward the wall. 'There's the phone. Why don't you call Phillips and have him pick us up?'

Peg reached down to the table. The keys jangled as she picked them up. She clutched them tightly to stop the noise. Then she opened her hand, and carefully studied them.

'What're you doing?' Jenny asked.

'There are keys here for two cars.'

'Hey! I'll bet the other's around here someplace!'

'Let's check the garage,' Peg said. 'We'll drive right out of Barlow, and keep on going.'

'Disneyland, here we come!'

Chapter Thirteen

Cordie glanced at the red numbers on her wristwatch. 'Okay, it's ten thirty. You guys are gonna leave now, right?'

'There's no point waiting any longer,' Robbins said.

'You're right.' Cordie took a deep, trembling breath. 'What're you gonna do, try and get to a road?'

'Eventually. We'll keep heading east and try to get out of Krull territory.'

'Yeah, well, good luck. You too, Ben.'

'Cordie?'

She wiped her sweaty hands on her jeans, and looked away. Ben took a step toward her. 'No. Don't, Ben. You go with the others.' She turned and ran. She heard quick footsteps, and knew that Ben was following. She ran harder. Damn it, he wasn't supposed to come. 'Go with *them*!' she called over her shoulder.

Reaching out, Ben grabbed her shoulder. He dragged her to a stop.

The others were out of sight.

'What do you want to do?' Ben asked, 'get yourself killed?'

'I can't leave. Mom and Dad are out here. I've got to find them.'

'I'll go with you, then.'

'No, don't.'

'I haven't got a choice, have I?'

'Go with the others. They're headed out. They've got a gun.'

'I can't.'

'Ben please.'

'I can't leave you. The same reason you can't leave your parents. I love you, I guess.'

'Oh Ben.' She pulled him tightly against herself. She kissed his mouth. Twisting a handful of his hair, she pulled back his head. 'I hope you don't regret it,' she muttered.

'I won't.'

'Let's find my folks and get our tails out of here.'

'This way,' Robbins said.

'Shouldn't we go after them?' Neala asked.

'They made their choice.'

'We're better off without them,' Sherri said.

'Come on.'

Neala, still with her back to the tree, squinted at the place in the darkness that had kept her filled with dread. She didn't move.

'Neala?'

'No, there's . . . Over there. Someone's hiding.'

'I'll check.'

'No!'

'Don't worry.' He walked toward the place unslinging his rifle and holding it ready.

'No! Don't, Johnny! Let's just go.'

He looked back at her. She thought she saw a smile on his face.

'Let's just go,' she said more softly.

'All right.' He turned away from the place Neala feared, and walked toward her.

She watched behind him. Her heart lurched as she glimpsed a quick movement. Something pale. A face? Whatever she'd seen, it vanished in an instant.

Johnny, seeing her alarm, looked back.

'It's nothing,' Neala said.

'You sure?'

Sherri stepped up beside Johnny, blocking Neala's view. 'What're we standing around for?'

Neala shook her head.

'I'll take up the rear,' Johnny said. 'We'll head east.' He pointed in the direction they'd been heading before they stopped. 'That way. Not much civilization out there, but we'll be okay once we get clear of Krull territory.'

'How far's that?' Sherri asked.

·'About twenty miles.'

'Oh shit.'

'Let's get started.'

'Neala pushed herself away from the tree. She glanced behind Johnny and Sherri, but saw nothing in the darkness.

She led the way. Sherri followed, staying close, and Johnny kept behind Sherri. At first, she ran too fast for the terrain. She tripped, and Sherri stumbled over her, stepping on her leg.

'You all right?' Sherri asked, gently helping her up.

I'll live.'

'Don't count on it.'

'Thanks a heap.'

Sherri patted her rump 'Think nothing of it.'

With Sherri in the lead, this time, they started running again. Neala ran more slowly than before. She tried to watch where her feet were landing, but the darkness hid all but glimpses of the ground.

The second time she tripped, she saw what did it.

A hand.

She yelped as she dived forward. The ground slammed her breathless. Rough hands turned her over, and a bony, white-skinned creature scurried up her body.

A man. A hairless man with the hollow face of a death's-head. He bit her mouth, and wetness dripped from his eyes.

Neala heard an awful thud. The head jerked away from her. The man flopped off, onto his back. She gazed at his erection, a loathsome thing like a rigid, pale snake. Then Johnny blocked her view. The rifle butt smashed into the horrible face, breaking through it.

'It's all right,' Johnny whispered. He helped her up.

Neala shook her head. She wiped tears from her eyes. Her shirt hung open, leaving her right breast uncovered. She closed the shirt. Not before noticing the fingernail scratches. They felt like burns on her skin.

'Did he hurt you?' Johnny asked.

'A little. I think I'm okay.'

'The filthy pig,' Sherri muttered. She stepped close to the body. 'Christ, look at him.'

Neala didn't.

'A fucking albino.'

Neala tried to fasten her shirt. The buttons were gone, so she overlapped the front and tucked it in.

'Shit,' Sherri said, still inspecting the body.

'We'd better get moving,' Johnny said.

Chapter Fourteen

In Tucker Grady's garage, they found a Dodge Dart. They went to its rear, and Jenny reached for the handle of the garage door.

'That won't work,' Peg told the girl. 'It's on remote control.'

'Oh no.'

'What's wrong with that?'

'It'll make enough racket to wake the dead – *and* the old woman.'

'Well?' Peg asked.

'We won't get any headstart if she starts screaming her head off or calls the cops or something. We'd better go in and tie her up.'

'My Lord, Jenny.'

'Come on, she's older than God. She can't hurt us.'

'Hadn't we better just get going?'

Jenny frowned at her. 'Do you want to blow everything?'

'I . . .'

'Let's take care of the old bat. Nothing to it.'

They left the garage, and re-entered the house through its back door. Jenny led the way through the kitchen and up a hallway so dark that Peg couldn't see her at all. Reaching out, she touched her daughter's back. She found Jenny's shoulder, and hung on.

'Right here,' Jenny whispered.

Peg heard a door moan open. Jenny moved sideways. Peg followed, her arm brushing the doorframe.

The room filled with light. Squinting against the sudden brightness, she saw Jenny's hand on the wall switch.

On the bed, an old woman was sitting upright, her eyes wide open, her bony arms held out. 'Took yer merry time,' she said in a high, brittle voice.

Jenny glanced around at Peg, confusion on her face.

'I knew you'd get to Heggie, one fine night. Felt it in my bones, I did. Don't know what kept you.'

Jenny walked toward the closet.

'Nobody there, young fella. I'm all alone. Been all alone since fifty-two when you took away my darling Brian.'

'What about Tucker?' Jenny asked.

'Took who? My Brian, my only Brian. You took him to yer trees. Oh Lord, you took him. You took him to yer trees.'

Jenny stepped into the closet and came out with a quilted robe.

'Took him for the dirty Krulls.'

She slipped a cloth belt off the robe, and walked toward the bed.

'I knew you'd come for me,' Heggie said, bobbing her head as Jenny tied her hands. 'I been waiting. I been figuring. I'll be a merry treat for the heathens.' She giggled. 'Trick or treat, trick or treat. Want to know my secret? Promise to keep mum?' She winked a pale eye at Jenny.

'Cross my heart,' the girl said loudly, and knotted the belt.

'Snake poison.' She giggled again. '*Rattlesnake* poison. Venom. Get it? I'm *full* of it. Full of it. Been dosing myself since fifty-two. Yessir. Full of it.' She hissed like a snake. 'Poison meat.'

Jenny glanced at Peg, fear in her eyes. Then she turned back to the old woman. 'We'll be right back.'

'Taking me to yer trees. Yessir. A merry treat for the dirty Krulls.'

Jenny hurried out of the bedroom. With a shaky hand, she brushed hair away from her forehead. Peg put a hand on her shoulder.

'She's nuts huh?'

'I guess so,' Peg said.

'Gosh.'

The garage door rumbled up, and Peg backed the Dodge down the driveway. She noticed Jenny looking toward the house. She looked, too. In one of the windows, a light was on. It must be the bedroom, she thought.

Jenny wrinkled her nose.

'What's wrong?'

'Crazy people. They make me nervous I guess.'

With a nod, Peg pulled onto the street. 'Better strap yourself in.'

'Do you really think she did it? Gave herself snake venom?'

Peg shrugged.

'I mean, that's weird. It's scary.' She snapped her seatbelt into place. 'Not a bad idea, though. Wonder where she keeps the snakes. I didn't see any around the house.' She opened the glove compartment. 'None in there.' She put one of her knives – the one she'd taken from her rear pocket before sitting in the car – into the glove compartment.

'Here, do something with these.'

Peg fumbled blindly on her lap, and picked up her two knives.

'Better keep one on you,' Jenny said.

'We won't need them now.'

'You never can tell.'

She handed one of the knives to Jenny, and left the other on her lap.

'Do you need the headlights?' Jenny asked.

Peg killed them. The pavement ahead went dark, but the street lamps gave enough light to steer by. She drove slowly, staying on Grove because it ran parallel to the highway. At the end of town, it stopped. She turned left, and stopped at the highway. Terk's Diner, on the corner, was closed for the night. Across the highway, the blue neon VACANCY sign of the Sunshine Motor Inn went dark, and blinked on again.

Far down the highway, headlights appeared. Peg's stomach knotted. She shifted to reverse and sped backwards, swinging the rear of the car toward the curb. She hit the brake pedal. The car jerked to a stop, and she turned off the engine.

'Get down!'

They both ducked low in their seats.

From the roar of the engine, she doubted that the approaching vehicle was a passenger car. It sounded more like a truck. She raised her head enough to peek out. A trailer truck plowed by.

Quickly, she started the engine and pulled onto the highway behind it.

'Los Angeles is *that* way,' Jenny protested.

'We'll worry about that later,' Peg said. 'Let's stay with the truck.'

She floored the gas pedal, trying to catch up, but the truck was too fast. It kept pulling away. She followed it around a curve, leaving Barlow behind. Without street lamps, she could barely see the road. She stayed in the middle of the highway. Soon, she found herself gaining on the truck. If she got close enough, she could simply follow in its wake, letting its taillights show her the way.

Its brake lights flashed on.

It slowed quickly. Peg moved up close behind it.

'It's gonna stop!' Jenny warned.

'My God, what . . . ?'

Steering across the center line, she saw lights ahead of the truck. Headlights. Parked cars. She swung behind the truck.

'A roadblock,' she muttered.

Jenny moaned.

Peg stepped on the brake. As the car jerked to a stop, she watched the truck pull slowly away.

'What'll we do?' Jenny asked.

She shook her head.

'They'll have it blocked the other way, too.'

'I know, I know.'

'Let's go back to Grady's.'

She wondered if she dare try Phillips. He might help. Or he might not. He claimed to love her, but . . .

'Oh geez, they've seen us!'

Stunned, Peg saw a car speed past the truck. Its headlights on high-beam, were blinding.

'Oh God!'

'Turn around!'

'It'll hit us!' she shrieked but her foot stomped the gas pedal and she jerked the steering wheel, swinging broadside to the onrushing car. She gritted her teeth, waiting for the impact as the force of the U-turn shoved her sideways. She straightened the wheel. Headlights burst in her rearview mirror. She mashed the accelerator. The car shook and bucked. She saw that her right tires were off the pavement. She eased left, bringing them onto the road.

'He's still gaining!' Jenny yelled. She was twisted around, looking out the rear window. 'He's right on our tail!'

She sped through the center of town, all its shops closed and dark, its only traffic signal blinking yellow. She shot beneath the light. Just ahead, a startled cat leaped and sprinted to safety.

'Stop!' Jenny said. 'Stop the car!'

'What?'

'We'll hit the other roadblock.'

'But . . .'

'Just stop.'

She took her foot off the gas. Slowly the car lost speed. The trailing car stayed close behind.

'We'll make *them* get out,' Jenny said. 'Whatever you do, don't get out. Do just what I say. There's only two of them, I think.'

As the car stopped, Jenny reached into the glove compartment. She took out the two knives, and gave one to Peg. The other, she slipped inside her blouse.

'Stick it in your armpit,' she said. 'Clamp your arm down.'

'I . . .'

The car pulled alongside. She recognized the boy in the passenger seat. Timmy Shaw. He met her eyes, then looked past her at Jenny and smiled. A vicious, mocking smile.

'Hi-ya Jenny,' he called.

As the car slid by, Peg opened a button and reached inside her dress top. She tucked the knife handle into her right armpit, and lowered her arm to hold the knife in place. Then she reached forward awkwardly to turn off the engine.

'Leave it going,' Jenny whispered.

The car stopped in front of them, and backed up until it bumped. Both doors opened. Jack Shaw climbed out the driver's side, and Timmy came out the other.

'Okay,' Jenny said. 'Back up, real quick, then run over the old guy.'

Peg turned to her daughter, shocked. 'I can't do that.'

'Geez Mom!'

'I just . . .!'

'They'll take us to the Trees!'

'But I . . .'

Shaw pulled open her door. 'Step on out, Mrs Stover.'

'You too,' the boy told Jenny.

Keeping her arm tight against her side, Peg climbed from the car. As she stood, she felt movement on her lap. The second knife! It hit the pavement with a clatter.

Shaw gazed at the knife. Then he smirked at Peg, shaking his head. 'Dumb,' he said, and smashed a fist into her belly.

She doubled. The road slammed her knees and she sprawled forward, sucking for air that wouldn't come.

Jenny, still sitting in the car, watched her mom go down.

'Come on,' Timmy muttered, grabbing the shoulder of her blouse.

'Leave go!'

He jerked her sideways. As she fell, she grabbed the door handle. The knife dropped from under her arm, slid down the in side of her blouse, and fell to the gravel. She let go of the door. She dropped to the ground, planning to reach for the knife.

Before she could move, the boy gripped her arms. He dragged her clear, gravel scraping her back. Then she felt the soft wetness of grass. She squirmed, trying to pull free. Timmy dropped onto her outstretched arms. His knees pounded like spikes into her arms, nailing them to the ground. After the first blast of pain faded, she felt his hands on her breasts.

'Timmy, what're you doing back there?'

The hands continued to rub and squeeze.

'Bring her over here.'

'In a minute,' Timmy called.

'Right now.'

He leaned farther forward, his hands sliding down her chest and belly. They tugged at her belt.

'Timmy!'

The boy unbuttoned her jeans. He slid the zipper down. Then he was lifted away and shoved aside.

'Damn it, you little twerp! We've got a job to do!'

'I only wanted a little feel,' he pouted.

Jenny rolled onto her side and drew her knees up.

'Just a feel, that's all.'

'Let's get her into the car,' the man said, sounding disgusted.

'Why don't we keep 'em, Dad?'

'You know better than that.'

'We could take 'em someplace and screw 'em.'

'And get the Krulls on us? Where's your brain, boy? Never mind, I *know* damn well – it's swinging between your legs.'

'Nobody'd have to know, Dad. We can kill 'em when we're done, and hide their bodies. I'd sure like to screw Jenny, Dad. Please?'

'Forget it. Now give me a hand.'

Kneeling, Timmy's father rolled Jenny onto her back. She opened her eyes. The broad, grim face was just above her. With a growl, she rammed the knife at his eye. It hit low, ripping open his face from cheekbone to chin.

He wailed. He grabbed his cheek and lurched

backward but Jenny caught his arm. She hung on and blindly stabbed overhead, the knife jolting as it hit bone. She struck again. This time, the blade went into softness. The man shrieked and fell.

Letting go, Jenny rolled off him. She glimpsed his gouting face and neck, then looked up at the boy.

Timmy's stunned eyes met hers. Then he spun around and ran. At the rear of the car, he tripped and fell sprawling.

Jenny saw her mother lying on the road, an arm outstretched.

'No!' Peg cried.

Jenny rushed past, ignoring her, and leaped onto Timmy.

The knife plunged. The boy squealed.

'No! That's enough! Don't *kill* him!'

The knife went down again.

Peg squirmed forward, dragging her useless legs, the cuffs on her ankle scraping along the pavement.

The boy stopped screaming.

Jenny raced by, knelt over Jack Shaw's body, and searched his pockets. Moments later, she was kneeling at Peg's feet.

'You . . . you didn't have to . . . slaughter them.'

'Didn't I?' Jenny asked, and unlocked the cuffs.

Chapter Fifteen

Cordie climbed onto the trunk of a fallen tree. She held a dead limb to steady herself, and gazed ahead. Nothing was visible in the darkness except more trees.

Ben climbed up beside her. 'Which way?' he asked.

'I guess it doesn't matter. I mean, they might be anywhere.' Cordie couldn't keep the despair out of her voice.

'Do you want to go back?'

'Go back where?'

'Try to find the others again.'

'Oh, you know right where they are?'

'Not exactly, but . . .'

'How the hell are we supposed to find them, then? Just turn around and start walking? That'll do a lot of good.' She sat on the trunk and scooted forward, her legs stretching toward the unseen ground. She pushed off. Not hard enough. A rough jutting stub of branch jabbed and scraped her back as she dropped. 'Damn!' She stumbled forward, grabbing at her back.

'You hurt?'

'Yes, Shit shit shit!'

Ben leaped down.

'God *damn*!'

'Let me see,' he said.

She turned away and lifted the back of her blouse.

'Its just a scratch.'

'Kiss it and make it well. But *gently*.' She felt the soft touch of his lips on her back.

'Better?'

'Yeah. Thanks.'

He stood beside her, and she took hold of his hand.

She studied the dark wilderness. 'I don't know, Ben. They might be anywhere.'

'We'll just keep going.' He shrugged. 'Not much else we can do.'

'If we could just find that clearing . . . I thought it was this way, but . . .' She shook her head. 'None of this looks familiar.'

'I don't think we've gone far enough, yet.'

'Maybe not.'

'It's a big clearing. We'll probably run into it.'

'I sup . . .'

She staggered back as a naked boy leaped from behind a tree. He planted himself in their way, crouching slightly, one hand forward. The hand held a knife. Cordie and Ben backed away, but the boy stepped forward, staying close to them.

'Run?' Ben whispered.

'Let's get his knife. He's just a kid.' Cordie lowered her eyes, hoping to spot something she could use as a weapon. The ground was too dark. But her heel knocked into a hard object. She stooped and felt for it. Her fingertips found a moist surface of bark. She grabbed, clutched a thick branch, and lifted. It started to pull free from the ground, but one end stayed down.

The damn thing was a dozen feet long!

As she let it go, the boy lunged. His knife flicked at her face. She threw out an arm to block it. The blade sliced into her forearm. Then Ben was on the boy, pulling him back, reaching for the knife hand. He couldn't get a grip on it, but Cordie grabbed the wrist with both hands. She twisted sharply. The arm made a sound like crackling gristle. The boy cried out. The knife fell.

Cordie dropped to her hands and knees while Ben struggled to hold the writhing boy. She raked the moist ground cover. Found the knife. Got to her feet. Braced herself. 'Okay, hold him.'

She pressed the point against the boy's belly. He stopped moving.

'Where do you live?' Cordie asked.

The boy growled. His upper lip curled, baring his teeth.

'I don't think he understands,' Ben said. 'Yeah. Maybe not.' She leaned close to the boy. 'Do you speak English?'

Again, the boy growled. 'The kid's an animal,' Ben muttered.

'Kid. I'm looking for my parents, my mom and dad. Do you know where they are? Where do you take the people you catch? Do you have a camp or something?'

'He can't talk.'

'What'll we do with him?' Cordie asked.

Ben shrugged. 'I don't know if we ought to let him go. No telling what he might do.'

'Well, I don't think I'm up to butchering him. Are you?'

'Ben sighed. 'I guess not.'

'Hey, let's have your belt. We can loop it around his neck, maybe use it like a leash, see where he takes us.'

'We can give it a try.'

Keeping one arm clamped around the boy's neck, Ben unfastened his belt and yanked it free. As he held it out to Cordie, she passed the knife to him.

She slipped the broad, leather tip through the buckle, and dropped the loop over the boy's head. Ben forced the belt down the thin neck. Cordie jerked it taut.

'Okay,' she said. 'Let him go and we'll see.'

Ben let go.

The boy leaped at Cordie. She sidestepped, tugging the belt, and swung him off his feet. He sprawled, choking. He clawed at his throat, but Cordie stepped on his back and kept the belt tight. He rolled. Cordie's foot skidded off. Balance lost, she fell. The belt flew from her hands.

She saw Ben kick. His shoe slammed into the boy's face, and the boy went down.

'He's out,' Ben said after nudging the body.

'Dead?'

'Just unconscious, I think.'

They took the time to bandage Cordie's cut arm.

Ben used the tail of his shirt, slicing it off with

the boy's knife and tying it around Cordie's wound.

Then Cordie knelt beside the boy. She loosened the belt. Touching his neck, she found his pulsebeat. 'Let's just leave him while he's still conked out,' she said.

'Fine with me.'

Leaving the boy, they ran through the trees. They had gone no more than fifty yard when a voice cried out the single word, 'Krull!'

Not the voice of the boy.

It came from behind. Cordie stopped, and turned.

'What was that?' she whispered.

'I don't . . .'

The shriek of the boy ripped into her ears.

Ben grabbed her arm. 'Come on.'

They ran a few steps. Then Cordie pulled free. 'Wait.' She crouched behind a tree and pulled Ben down beside her. 'What'd that sound like?' she whispered.

'Like a maniac.'

'I mean, didn't it sound like somebody yelled, "Krull," and then maybe killed the kid?'

'Sure did.'

'Maybe he'll help us.'

'You're nuts.'

'No really. I mean, *we're* not Krulls. Maybe he's trying to get away from here too, just like us.'

'Not just like us. You heard him, for Christsake. He hardly sounded human.'

'It'd be . . .' Her voice froze in her throat as she heard the quiet crushing of underbrush.

Ben's hand tightened in hers.

A tall, broad shape strode between the trees. In one hand, it held a machete. From the other swung the head of the boy.

A strangled whimper escaped from Cordie.

Ben lunged away, pulling her hand. She jerked it free. Ben glanced back.

The awful voice roared, '*Krull*!

Ben ran.

Cordie staying down saw dark shape after him.

Then there was only forest. She heard the crashing footfalls.

Ben yelled, 'No! Please!'

She covered her ears.

Ben's final cry was cut short.

She curled at the base of the trunk, and hugged her knees, and listened to the woods.

Chapter Sixteen

'Holy shit, a cabin!'

Robbins caught up to Neala. They stopped beside Sherri, and looked through the trees.

Near the end of a long, moon-washed clearing stood a cabin of logs.

'Not bad,' Robins said. 'Let's have a look.'

He went first, stepping into the open and pausing to scan the area. The clearing was larger than a football field. Watching the edges of the forest, he saw no movement. The cabin looked dark and deserted. 'Stay close,' he said.

Neala stepped to his right side, Sherri to his left. He started forward, rifle ready. The ground felt springy under his boots. A cool breeze stirred across his bare arms.

He looked at Neala. She was limping. Her mouth was pressed shut as if she were biting into the pain. She looked very brave and very vulnerable. He wanted to hold her.

She saw him looking, and made a smile.

'How're the feet?' he asked.

'They've seen better nights.'

He turned to Sherri. 'Gonna make it?'

'First chance I get,' she said, and laughed sourly.

As they moved closer to the cabin, Robbins saw that it stood in a field of pickets. Each of the tall poles had a crossbar like the armbones of a scarecrow. Each was topped with a dark ball.

Sherri grabbed his arm and pulled him to a halt. 'Oh shit,' she gasped. 'Oh fucking shit!'

'They're *heads*,' Neala whispered.

Robbins squinted at the top of the nearest pole. The sphere on top was a head, all right, its dark hair drifting in the breeze. He looked from one pole to another. A head was impaled on each. 'Good God,' he said. He took a step forward.

Sherri tugged his arm. 'We're not going in there!'

He turned to Neala.

She shook her head, her face twisted with disgust.

'The cabin,' he said.

'I don't want to,' Neala told him in a voice like a terrified child.

. Turning around, he saw movement in the woods. A face appeared beside an aspen. He raised his rifle and took aim, but the face slipped sideways. It vanished behind the trunk.

To the left, a pale body darted between trees.

Sherri groaned loudly.

'Let's go for the cabin,' Robbins said.

Neala squeezed his arm.

A knife arched through the night, flipping end over end, its blade flashing moonlight. Robbins shoved Neala. She stumbled sideways as the knife whipped by. Robbins rushed to her.

'Let's go,' he said, pulling her up.

'God, it would've . . . '

114

'It didn't.'

They raced toward the cabin. Sherri caught up. A dozen feet before the first stake, Robbins dropped Neala's arm and snatched the knife from the ground. 'Take this,' he said. He looked back.

He saw no one.

Then he led the way among the poles, ducking beneath the cross-bars. The pikes were close together. He moved carefully, afraid of bumping them, but his rifle butt knocked into one. The staff wobbled. Something dropped from above and Neala, behind him, gasped with horror. He wanted to look around, but the staffs enclosed him like a cage. He couldn't turn without tipping others.

'You all right?' he called back.

No answer.

'Neala?'

'I'm okay,' she whispered.

'Sherri?'

'*Get us out of here!*'

'How's the rear?' The words were out before he realized his mistake. 'Forget . . .'

'*Yaaaaah!*'

He raised himself. His shoulder hit a cross-bar. The staff wobbled in the loose earth. He clutched it to stop it from falling. Then he pivoted and looked back. Neala was still crouched low. Sherri, a distance behind her, was standing upright, back toward him, shoulders level with the cross-bars, head just below the other heads. Robbins watched her, and knew she wasn't checking the rear for Krulls. She was gazing at the impaled heads.

Dozens of them. Surrounding her. Pressing close like a hideous mob.

'Sherri!' he shouted.

She whirled around. Knocked into a pole. It fell against another, and that one tipped, and suddenly a dozen staffs were swaying and falling, their grisly ornaments jerking toward each other as if to share a secret, others thudding together, some falling and rolling.

Sherri looked at it all, then at Robbins. Her eyes and mouth were dark holes in her moonlit face.

Neala started to rise. Robbins pushed her head down. 'Don't look,' he said.

'Sherri, just come on forward.'

She didn't move.

'Sherri!'

'I can't.'

'Stay right here,' he said to Neala.

Crouching below the cross-bars, he made his way through the forest of pikes. When he got close to Sherri, he found the crosses standing at crazy angles. He tried to lift one out of the way. A weathered head, little more than a skull with patches of hair trailing in the breeze, wobbled in front of his face. Sickened, he dropped the pike.

He stood facing Sherri. She was several feet away.

A tangle of sticks and heads separated them. Keeping his eyes on her, he began moving forward, stepping high, his boots smashing the frail crosses to the ground. Twice, he stepped on heads. One crushed. The other tipped like a rock and nearly sent him sprawling. He caught his balance, choked with horror at the thought of falling into such things.

Then he had Sherri by the arm.

He looked beyond her. Nobody was in pursuit.

'You all right?'

She answered with a whimper.

Holding her arm, he pulled her through the trampled mesh.

'Shut your eyes,' he said. He looked back to make sure they were shut. Then he pulled her forward again. He told her to hold onto his belt. When he reached the first upright cross, he kicked it aside. The head flew off, but he didn't watch. Another cross stood in his way. Cursing, he used his rifle butt to knock it aside. He moved fast, smashing the barriers down.

'Neala, keep your eyes shut. We're coming up behind you.'

He slammed the sticks out of his way. They crashed into others, heads flying.

When he was close to Neala, he uprooted three of the crosses and flung them to the sides. He stepped past her. 'Grab onto Sherri. Keep your eyes shut and hang on.'

'Johnny, what . . .?'

'I'm getting us to that cabin.'

He shot his foot forward, kicking down a frail stick. It took down the one in front of it, and that one tore down another. As they fell, he plowed ahead and knocked down more. He swung his rifle. The butt smashed through one cross after another. He swung high and it clubbed a head. He swept low. The pikes scattered. Then there were no more in front of him. The cabin door was yards away.

Robbins turned, and saw the path he'd battered through the barrier. The passage was bordered by half-fallen crosses that teetered at strange angles.

'It's all right,' he said.

The women stood and looked back. Sherri covered her mouth. Neala quickly turned away.

Robbins walked to the cabin door. It had no knob. A leather thong hung out.He pulled it, and heard a squeak of wood inside as the latch lifted. He pushed the door. It swung open.

'Hello?' he called into the darkness.

No answer came.

He stepped through the doorway. The air smelled gamey. It felt warm and damp. He peered through the darkness. He could see nothing.

Reaching into his pants pocket, he found his book of matches. He flipped open the cover, tore a match loose, and struck it. The head flared. He squinted against the sudden brightness, and turned in a full circle. Satisfied no one was lurking in the small room, he shook out the match and returned to the door.

'It's okay. Come on in.'

Neala and Sherri entered. Robbins pulled the door shut, cutting off the moonlight. The wooden latch dropped into place. He struck another match. In its fluttering light, he quickly searched for a lamp. He found a candle holder protruding from a wall, and lit it. Each wall had a candle. He lit them all. Their tips fluttered, filling the room with shadows.

'Must be a bed,' Sherri muttered, looking down at a nest of fur pelts. She sat on it, rubbed her hands cautiously over the top, then lay back and sighed.

Neala stood in the center of the room. She turned slowly. Her eyes moved up to Robbins' face.

'I think we should get out of here,' she said.

'We need the rest,' Robbins said. 'This place'll be easy to defend.'

Sherri raised her head. 'I'm not going out there again.'

'But . . .' Neala nervously rubbed her mouth. 'Whoever lives here, he must be the one who put up the heads.'

'I don't want to hear this,' Sherri said.

'What if he comes back?'

Chapter Seventeen

Art Phillips came to the door in his boxer shorts. 'Peg?' he asked.

She stepped into the dark foyer, Jenny close behind. Art shut the door. He turned on a bright overhead light, and gaped at them. '*Jesus* what happened?'

'We're in trouble,' Peg said.

'I can see that.' He shook his head, frowning, and rubbed one eye. His hair was mussed from sleep. 'What kind of trouble? Come on in here, let's sit down. *Jesus*!'

They followed him into the living room. Peg stared at his pale, freckled back. His shorts hung low, showing the cleavage of his rump. Only two days ago, she'd hooked a finger into that groove, and tugged his shorts down. He'd fallen onto his bed, the shorts around his knees, and rolled onto his back, and she'd taken him into her mouth . . . Only two days ago. And yet, she was afraid now to ask him for help.

He turned to Jenny. 'Is that blood?'

Jenny nodded.

'Are you hurt?'

She smiled strangely. 'It's not my blood.'

'Whose?'

'Ask Mom.'

'Do you want to go wash up?' he asked her. 'Take a shower, why don't you?'

'Okay. Thanks.'

He pointed the way to the bathroom, and rubbed the back of his head as he watched her leave.

'Now what happened, Peg?'

'I left Hank.'

'What do you mean? Here, sit down.' He dropped onto the couch, and patted the cushion beside him. Peg sat down. He rubbed the back of her neck.

'I decided to run away from Hank, tonight. But he caught me and Jenny sneaking out. He . . . He was hurting Jenny. I had to stop him. He kept beating on her . . . I think I killed him.'

'*You killed Hank?*'

'I stabbed him,' she said. She found it easy to lie. Art continued to stroke her neck. He said nothing. Peg could hear the distant spray of the shower.

'Where were you planning to go?' he finally asked.

'Just away. Los Angeles, maybe.'

'Are you nuts? You can't leave Barlow.'

'I *killed* him, Art.'

'There're other ways. Plead self-defense or something. You can't leave Barlow. That's suicide.'

'Not if you help us.'

He quickly took his hand off her neck. 'No way.'

'With your security pass . . .'

'That won't do you any good. Not if they're looking for you. They'll have roadblocks at each end of town . . .'

'They already do. Jenny had an idea, though. We could hide in the trunk of your car. They wouldn't look in the trunk, would they?'

'They might.' He leaned back, folding his hands behind his head, and stared at the ceiling. 'You've really done it to me.'

'I know. I'm sorry.'

'If I don't turn you in, and anyone finds out you were here . . .'

'Nobody has to know.'

'They'll know, all right. And then they'll come after me.'

'That's the whole thing, Art. Leave with us, and never come back. They can't hurt you, then. You haven't got any family. You'll be free and safe, and you'll never have to worry about the Krulls again. Wouldn't you like that? Aren't you tired of living in fear?'

'Don't give me that "living in fear" shit. Don't you watch the news? That world out there is full of maniacs. Jesus, they kill you for no reason. Nobody's safe out there. It ain't like that in Barlow. You can walk around the block, here, without getting snatched or raped or your brains blown out. You don't have to lock your doors at night to keep all the freaks out. So don't tell me about living in fear. You got nothing to worry about, here in Barlow, as long as you play by the rules.'

'But if you break the rules . . .'

'Then you're up shit creek.'

She stared down at her folded hands. They felt cold and heavy on her lap. 'Is it true, what they say about the Krulls?'

'Depends what you heard.'

'Oh God, Art!' Her hands blurred as tears filled her eyes and she began to cry, hunching over and sobbing loudly.

Art stroked her back. 'Take it easy,' he said. 'Hey, come on take it easy. Nothing to cry about.'

'I'm . . . Oh God, I'm so frightened!'

'Hey, don't cry.'

'If you won't help . . . Jenny's so . . . she's just a child. How can you . . . how can you do that to her?'

'Do what?'

'Give her to the Krulls.'

'Look, turn yourself in. Plead self-defense. Everyone knows what a bastard Hank was. You'll get acquitted, and that'll be that. You don't have to worry about the Krulls, at all. They haven't got a thing to do with it, if you just forget this dumb idea of running away.'

'You don't understand,' she sobbed.

'Look, give John a call. He'll tell you.'

'I can't. He's . . . He went to the Trees, tonight.'

'I know. I was with him.'

'No, I mean later. He went back.'

'What?' Art asked, his voice suddenly low and hard.

'He went back to free some girl.'

'You're kidding.'

124

'That's why . . . why we have to leave.'

'That idiot!' he snapped. 'That damned idiot! I *knew* he wasn't right, tonight. The way he kept sticking up for that gal. I knew something was off. What on earth could . . . how could he *do* a thing like that? Put you on the line like that? And Jenny? My God didn't he know he was cutting your throats?'

'He planned to come for us.'

'But he didn't.'

'Peg shrugged. 'He might've. He had to go before . . .'

'No. No way. The Krulls got him, sure as hell. And now they'll want you and Jenny. The immediate family.'

'Are we "immediate family"?'

'You're all John's got. They have to set an example, and you're it.'

'It isn't fair.'

'So what is? I'm sorry, Peg. I'm really sorry.'

He got up from the couch. Peg lifted her head. She wiped the tears from her eyes. 'You won't help us?'

'I wish I could, hon.'

'I thought you . . . cared for me.'

'I do. I like you a lot, you know that. But you can't expect me to throw my life away, can you?'

'If you drive us out and don't come back . . .'

'No way.' He stepped across the room to the telephone.

Peg's shaking hands fumbled with the buttons of her dress.

'None of that, now.'

She stood and walked slowly toward him, working on the buttons.

'Come on, don't make a fool of yourself.' He picked up the phone and looked down to dial.

Peg reached inside her dress. The knife lay loose at her side, held up by her tight belt. She gripped its handle.

Art began to dial.

She pulled out the knife. 'Stop,' she said.

Art saw the knife. He smirked, and kept on dialing. 'Put that down,' he said, 'before I take it away and make you eat it.'

'Put down the phone,' said another voice.

He looked past Peg.

She turned her head, and saw Jenny in the hallway. The girl's face and clothes were still dark with dried blood. In her hand was a big, bedroom pillow.

In the background, the shower continued to run with a sound like leaves in a strong wind.

'I took a look around,' Jenny said. She grinned with one side of her face. 'Guess what I found.'

'Hey now,' Art muttered. He put down the telephone.

'You were going to turn us in, you creep.'

'No, I . . .'

A muffled shot stopped his words. The pillow jerked. A hole blossomed in its white case, spouting feathers.

With a yell, Art grabbed his left forearm.

'No!' Peg cried. She rushed toward him.

'Mom, get away!'

'No! I won't let you kill him, I won't let you! No!'

126

'For gosh sakes, Mom.'

Art fell to his knees, whimpering.

Peg, standing in front of him, stared at her daughter. Jenny dropped the pillow. In her hand was a small, nickle-plated automatic.

'All right,' Jenny said. 'I'll keep him covered, and you tie him up. Gag him, too.'

Chapter Eighteen

Neala sat under a candle, her back against a wall, and watched Johnny search the cabin.

He checked the walls first. They were hung with deer skins, probably to keep the winds out. He lifted each pelt, and looked beneath it.

When he finished the walls, he stepped to the fireplace. A black pot hung over the dead coals. He swung it out, took off the lid, and sniffed. Gagging, he jammed the lid into place.

Sherri, asleep on her pile of furs, groaned and rolled onto her side.

'What is it?' Neala whispered to Johnny.

'Spoiled.'

He returned the pot to its hook. He pushed his hand into the ashes beneath it. 'Cold,' he said. Brushing off his hand, he stood. He hefted a metal fireplace poker. It looked solid and heavy to Neala. He swung it a few times as if testing its weight, then put it back. For a few moments, he inspected the sooty billows, a broom, a stool with a wicker seat. Then he turned away.

He wandered the cabin floor, his feet silent on the thick layers of fur that covered it.

'What're you looking for?' Neala asked.

'Anything we can use.' He shook his head. 'The place is bare. Except for that.' He nodded toward the covered pot.

'What do we need?'

'Food and water. A couple of guns would be nice.'

From the corner came Sherri's voice. 'While you're dreaming, how about a chopper to haul us the fuck outa here?'

'Maybe there's another room,' Neala suggested.

'I already checked. No other doors.'

'Another shack? Out back, maybe?'

'I'll take a look.' He went to the door, picked up his rifle, and raised the latch. He pulled the door open.

His body was a black, strong shape against the pale darkness outside. He seemed alert and dangerous, peering into the night. Then he glanced back. 'See you later,' he said, and Neala heard in his voice the bravery of a frightened boy.

He reached in to pull the door shut.

'Just a second,' Neala said.

He waited while she got to her feet and joined him outside.

Her eyes wandered over the dozens of frail crosses and heads. She saw the path Johnny had battered through them.

'Let's go around back,' Johnny said.

They walked close to the cabin. At its corner, Neala saw more crosses, more heads. At the rear, still more. But no other buildings. The small, square cabin stood alone.

They completed the circle, and stopped by the door.

'I'll stay out for a while,' Johnny said. 'You go on in and get some sleep.'

Neala hesitated. Maybe the man wanted time by himself. More likely, though, he was just trying to be nice, offering to stand guard while she slept.

'I want to stay with you,' she said.

'Well . . .'

'If you want to be alone . . .'

'No, it's all right.' He grinned. 'You think I want to be alone with all this?' He eyed the field of heads. 'What if they start talking to me?'

'Do you think they might?'

'Not if we keep the conversation up.'

'Can we sit down?'

They sat on the ground. Neala crossed her ankles, and leaned back against the logs of the cabin. They felt scratchy through her shirt. She kept her eyes down as she talked. 'I want to thank you,' she said. 'I don't know what's going on, or why you did it, but you saved our lives.'

'Well . . .'

She waited for him to continue, but he said nothing more. 'Why *did* you come back for us?'

'Who knows?'

'You must.'

'Yeah. I guess I do.'

'Tell me.'

'I guess I didn't want to see you die.'

She eased sideways until she felt him against her shoulder. She was strongly attracted to this man; it confused her. He was part of the scheme that brought her into this nightmare. Perhaps she ought to loathe him for that. She couldn't. He was powerful and deadly, but vulnerable in a way that made her want to hold him close.

'Why me?' she asked.

'I don't know. There's something . . . I knew what they'd do to you. The thought of you being hurt . . .'

'What about Sherri? Suppose I hadn't been along. Would you have left her to be killed?'

'Yes.'

'Why?'

'It's the way things are done in Barlow. It's the way we've always done things from the start.'

'How did it start?' She looked at him. He met her eyes, then turned away to scan the area.

'I'm not sure anyone knows,' he said. 'Apparently, the Krulls were here first. Nobody seems to know where they came from. Plenty of theories, though. Some say they're the Devil's children, some say a stone-age tribe of some kind.'

'If they're stone-age, where'd they get the steel weapons?'

'From us. We give them what they want. Except guns.'

Neala shook her head.

'Anyway. My high school history teacher had a theory that the Krulls are descendents of a band of Vikings that came up the Pacific coast and worked their way up the delta.'

'What do you think?'

'I think they might've descended from some crazy old mountain man – a demented Daniel

Boone.' She saw a wry grin as he shrugged. 'What the hell, nobody knows. I've got a neighbor, Joanne Early, who thinks they're Martians. Whatever they are, they're in control. They used to raid town about once a month, but then our forefathers got smart and started delivering strangers to them. That worked out nicely, because the townspeople robbed the folks before taking them out.'

'They're still at it,' Neala said, looking down at one of her bare, bloody feet.

'Both sides get something out of it. And as long as the Krulls get eight or ten victims a month, they leave us alone.'

'Hasn't anyone ever tried to stop them?'

'There've been a few attempts. Not many, though. A fellow named MacQuiddy went in, once, with a bunch of men from town. They called themselves the Glorious Fourteen. That was back in the thirties. For a time, back then, word was out that Barlow was a good place to avoid. Travelers stopped coming through, and our people stopped taking victims out to the forest. So the Krulls came into town, one night. They snatched a dozen of our women and children. The Glorious Fourteen went in to rescue them, and never came out.'

Neala watched his eyes roam over the field of heads. 'Nobody ever comes out,' he said.

'Will we?'

'We'll sure give it a try.' Johnny put an arm across her shoulders, and she leaned her head against him.

She felt good, being with Johnny.

Better than she'd felt with any man since Derek. That was nearly two years ago. The break-up had left her stunned. She spent six months living like a hermit: hating Derek, hating all men, yet dwelling on the times they'd had together and dreaming of his return as if she enjoyed the twist of pain that such thoughts brought to her.

When the loneliness finally drove her from the house, she met only desperate men. They wanted her body close to them in the night, because they had the loneliness, too. Many tried to be cool: they talked big, and drove Porsches, and pretended. Others displayed their sensitivity like a raw wound, whiners pleading for attention. Few and far between were the normal guys, the confident ones she might want to know better.

She suspected most were already married – busy raising children and dogs.

And now, here was Johnny Robbins. You couldn't say he was normal, not after growing up in a town like Barlow and doing the terrible things he'd done. But he was strong and confident. He could be gentle. And he spoke straight.

He was so different from those other men – so solid, someone to rely on.

Someone she might love.

Her eyes filled with tears. She sniffed, and Johnny looked at her.

'I'm sorry,' she said.

'Don't be sorry.'

'It's just all so horrible.'

'I know.' His hand stroked her hair, the side of her wet face.

'We'll never get a chance to know each other, Johnny. I mean, to spend time and do things.'

'We'll get the chance,' he said.

She shook her head. A sob wracked her body.

'We will. You can count on it.'

His face moved close to hers. He looked into her eyes, and smiled gently, and pressed his mouth to hers.

Chapter Nineteen

Cordie lay on the ground, curled up and shivering at the foot of the tree, afraid to move. She stayed that way for a long time.

Hours must have passed since she'd seen the dark shape stride through the trees. Hours since she'd heard Ben's pleading, terrified voice. God, he must've died an awful death.

The thing had come her way, and passed her by.

But it might be lurking near.

She couldn't stay on the ground much longer. She had to urinate badly, and she didn't want to wet herself.

Finally, she rolled onto her belly. She raised her head. Her eyes searched the forest. The air had a blue-gray cast, and she could see a long distance into the surrounding timber.

With sudden dread, she realized that the night's protective darkness was gone.

She got to her knees. Her right arm, numb from being crushed by her body for so long, hung useless at her side. Slowly, feeling returned to the arm. It tingled and burned. She shook it. She flexed her fingers. When the arm felt usable again, she stood up.

She turned slowly, studying the woods. She seemed to be alone.

Quickly, she lowered her pants and squatted. Her stream sounded terribly loud hitting the leafy ground. Eyes on the woods, she wished the noise would end. But she wasn't willing to stop the flow; getting rid of the aching tightness felt so good. Finally, she finished. She stood and pulled up her pants.

For a few moments, she stared in the direction that Ben had run. She didn't want to see his body. She couldn't just leave, though. Not without knowing, for sure, that he was dead. To know with absolute certainty, she had to see him.

She walked slowly, trying to move with total silence. In spite of her care, each footstep caused a quiet crush of the forest debris. Not much of a sound. But enough for others to hear. Too much. She took longer strides. Though her footsteps were louder, that way, she wouldn't need as many to reach her goal.

A goal she didn't want to reach. She wanted only to hide.

But she *had* to find out.

She kept moving. She knew just where to look. All night, in her mind, she had seen Ben dart into the trees, heard him running, heard his voice. He hadn't gone far. No farther than the distance, back home, between the front door and the kitchen.

When she saw his legs, she stopped. He was on his back, one leg straight out, the other bent sideways at the knee in a position that looked painful. The rest of Ben was hidden behind a tree.

His pants were all covered with blood.

'Ben?' she asked. The word came out as quiet as a breath.

But much too loud.

She took a step, and saw more: the lap of his pants, the bloody stomach of his shirt. She inched closer. The tree uncovered more: his chest, his outflung right arm. With another step, she would see if . . .

No!

She took a step backward until the tree concealed all but his legs. She stared at them. They were blurred by her sudden tears.

Those shoes.

She'd flung one out the car window at a drive-in movie, last week.

'Oh Ben,' she moaned.

Then she ran. She knew she was making too much noise, but she didn't care.

Let them get me. *Let* them!

She ran hard. Away from Ben. Running blindly, tears in her eyes, head thrown back. Better to look at the sky, the blue morning sky, than whatever might be coming to kill her.

She crashed into a thicket. Its limbs gripped her legs, but she churned through, kicking and grunting. It couldn't hold her back. As she broke free, though, it caught her trailing foot. It tripped her. She plunged forward, shrieked, and twisted wildly to keep from falling onto a naked boy.

The boy who'd attacked her last night.

The one slaughtered only minutes before Ben.

She hit the ground. Got to her hands and knees. Glanced at the body. Saw blood and ants, and the pulpy stump of neck where his head should have been.

Scrambling to her feet, she ran. She knew she was making too much noise.

Now, she cared.

As soon as she was well away from the body, she stopped. She looked around.

There!

A dense thicket, off to the right.

She rushed to the high cluster of bushes. She circled it, trying to see inside. The closely packed, leafy branches blocked her view.

Perfect!

Dropping onto her belly, she squirmed forward. She pushed her way through leaves and springy, low-hanging tendrils. Deeper and deeper into the thicket.

Finally, she stopped. She looked to each side, and saw no hint of the outside world. She rolled. Directly above, she could see a few tiny patches of sky.

Something tickled her arm.

She looked.

An ant.

Her fingertip got it. The ant left a tiny smear on her skin.

'Not yet,' she muttered.

140

Chapter Twenty

Neala woke up. Her head was on Johnny's lap. They were still outside, Johnny sitting with his back to the cabin wall.

He smiled down at Neala. His eyes were bloodshot. His face, dark with a day's growth of whiskers, was torn by scratches and streaked with the brown stains of dry blood.

Reaching up, she touched his rough cheek.

'Guess I could use a shave,' he said.

'And sleep. Did you get any sleep at all?'

'What's sleep?'

His hand caressed Neala's forehead. It felt big and warm and comforting. She drew it down to her mouth, and kissed it. Then she slipped it inside her shirt. She closed her eyes as the hand moved lightly over her breasts. It stroked the skin of her belly. She felt his hardness push against the back of her head. The hand returned to her breasts, less gentle now, squeezing and plying her rigid nipples.

She moved his hand away, and stood. Her stiff muscles ached and burned as she stretched. She smiled down at Johnny. He watched as if he knew what would happen next.

She opened her shirt, and slipped it off.

'Are you sure?' Johnny asked. 'Here?'

She kept her eyes on Johnny. If she turned to the field of impaled heads, she knew she could not go through with it. 'Here's the only place we have,' she said.

'Inside.'

'Sherri.' She tugged at her belt and opened it. 'Here's fine. In the sunlight.' She unfastened her corduroys, and slid them down her legs. Stepping out of them, she stood before Johnny, clad only in her brief panties. She slipped them off. The morning breeze licked her skin. The sun was warm.

Neala opened her eyes when the cabin door squeaked open. Sherri stepped out.

'You done?' Sherri asked, her voice sarcastic.

'For Godsake!'

'Oh, don't pay any attention to me.'

'Get out of here! What's the *matter* with you!'

Shaking her head, Sherri gazed into the distance. 'Nothing's the matter with *me*. I just wonder about you two.'

'If you'll go inside for a minute,' Johnny said, 'we'll finish up and get dressed.' His voice was calm.

'Don't you like an audience?'

'Damn it, Sherri!'

'Well, you've got one. Just thought I'd let you know.' She pointed.

Neala turned her head. 'Oh God,' she moaned. She gripped Johnny's sides.

'They've been out there since you started,'

142

Sherri said. 'Just a couple, at first. Must be fifteen or twenty now. I guess they liked the show.'

Johnny raised himself. He was still inside her, still erect. With a look of tenderness and regret, he slowly slid out. Moving on his knees, he grabbed his rifle. He stood, shouldered it, and aimed toward the scattered group beyond the barrier of heads.

Neala began to gather the cast-off clothes. She glanced up. Sherri was staring at her. 'Give me a hand, damn it!'

Nodding, Sherri crouched and picked up Johnny's boots, his socks, his pants. That took care of it. Neala rushed ahead of her into the cabin.

Sherri stopped in the doorway, and looked out. She stayed in the doorway as Johnny moved toward it.

Dropping her bundle of clothes, Neala grabbed Sherri's arm and tugged her inside.

Sherri swung around. 'Leave me alone!'

'Sherri, for Godsake, you're acting . . .'

Sherri clutched Neala's hair and jerked her head back. 'Shut up,' she hissed. 'Just shut your fucking mouth!'

Chapter Twenty-one

'I'll take the gag off,' Peg said. 'But you have to promise not to yell.'

Art nodded.

Peg set down the .22 automatic, and got up from the kitchen table. She stepped behind Art. Crouching, she checked the ropes binding his hands and feet to the metal chair. They were secure.

She picked a corner of the wide tape loose from the side of his face, got a firm grip, and tugged. The tape peeled off. Opening his mouth, Art worked the handkerchief forward. Peg pinched the wet ball of cloth and removed it.

'Thanks,' he gasped. 'Can I have a drink?'

'I suppose.'

'Coffee.'

She stepped over to the cupboard and reached up for a coffee mug.

'I'm sure sorry about last night,' he said.

'I'll bet you are.' She poured coffee into the mug, and added a tablespoon of sugar. At the refrigerator, she put in a splash of cream.

'I am sorry,' he said. 'I was just so shocked, you know? I wasn't thinking.'

Peg lifted the mug to his mouth. He sipped from it. She tilted it higher. Coffee spilled from its corners and streamed down his chin.

'Sorry,' she mumbled.

Flustered, she put down the mug. She grabbed a napkin and wiped the trails of wetness from his chin, his neck, his chest. Spots had even dribbled onto his lap. His penis showed through the slit of his boxer shorts. Quickly, Peg stepped away.

'Jenny would've killed me,' he said.

'I know.'

'You saved my life.'

'I'm not sure why.'

'I owe you, Peg.'

'What's that supposed to mean?'

'It means I'll do what you asked. I'll drive you and Jenny out of here.'

'I don't know.'

'Well *Jesus*, isn't that what you want?'

'I'll have to ask Jenny.'

'*Ask* her?'

'She's better at these things than me.'

'She's a kid. What does she know?'

'She seems to know a lot about surviving.'

'Okay. So ask her.'

'She's sleeping.'

'Wake her up. You want to get out of here don't you?'

'I think I'll just let her sleep. She'll wake up in due time.'

'Let me have some more coffee then, okay?'

Peg stepped again to the table, and lifted the

146

mug. 'We'll take it slow and easy this time,' she said.

This time, not a drop spilled.

'Thanks, hon,' Art said. 'You know, if you really wanted to help me, you'd let me out of this chair.'

'Oh sure.'

'It's been hours. My arm's just killing me.'

'Your arm's hardly scratched.'

'That's easy for you to say, you're not the one who's shot.'

'I bandaged it, Art. I saw it. It's nothing. A scratch.'

'It hurts like hell.'

'Well, you'll just have to live with it.'

'You're gonna have to untie me, anyway.'

'Oh why's that?'

'How else am I gonna drive you and Jenny out of here?'

Chapter Twenty-two

Waking up, Cordie stared through the tangled roof of bushes. She listened, afraid to move.

She heard running. She heard the jabber of voices. She heard harsh laughter. From the sounds, she guessed that half a dozen teenaged kids were nearby.

The thicket no longer felt like a refuge. Now it was a trap.

She wanted to get out, to run . . .

They might hear her, though. They might hear her crawling over the matted leaves and twigs, and get to her before she was free. Trapped in the mesh of bushes, she would be helpless. A game for the kids.

Play with her.

Taunt her, cut her, set her on fire.

She listened to their vicious laughter, their squeals.

All around the thicket.

As if they knew she was there.

She wanted to curl up on her side and hug her knees to her breasts. She didn't dare. Instead, she pressed her legs tightly together. She pressed her arms to her sides. She stared at the morning sky through a cross-work of limbs.

And waited.

The kids argued in sharp, high voices. Someone chuckled. Bushes rustled.

Cordie's rigid body trembled. Her neck ached with stiffening muscles.

They know I'm here!

How *could* they?

She heard the sounds of someone crawling inside the thicket. Coming for her.

She sucked in her breath and held it, trying not to scream.

All other sounds stopped.

They're listening, she thought. They're all out there listening, waiting.

Cordie raised her head. She looked down her body, past her shoes, and saw a face appear. The face of a girl. A blonde girl with twigs in her wild hair. A girl with blood smeared on her lips, her cheeks, her chin.

She was young. Fourteen or fifteen. Her tanned shoulders were bare.

As the girl crawled closer, Cordie heard herself gulping quick short breaths. Swallowing, she choked and gasped for air.

The girl moved alongside Cordie. The skin of her back was cross-hatched with scratches and smudges of dirt. Her buttocks were bleeding from scratches like the rake-marks of fingernails.

She sat up and crossed her legs. 'I'm Lily,' she said. 'What's your name?'

Cordie mumbled her name.

'What?'

'Cordelia.'

'That's a weirdo name.' She wrinkled her nose. 'What kind of weirdo name is that?'

'Who *are* you?'

'Lily.'

'You're one of *them*?'

'Sure.' Lily scratched one of her breasts. 'I've been with 'em a couple of years. It's fun.'

'Fun?'

'Shit yes!' She giggled. 'No school, nobody telling you what to do, fucking all the time. It's great. You'll like it.'

Cordie shook her head.

'You'll love it, really.'

'You're murderers.'

'Sure. It's a gas. Anyway, you're suppose to come out.'

'What for?'

The girl smiled and shrugged. 'You don't want to stay in here.' Leaning forward, she propped her elbows on her knees. She whispered, 'If you don't come out, the boys, they'll have to come *in*. They won't like that. They'd have to crawl. So you'd better just come out with me.'

Cordie shook her head.

'They'll get real mad. It'll spoil your chance.'

'Chance of what?'

'Joining up. They just won't let you, if they're pissed.'

'What happens if I join up?'

'Then we don't kill you.'

'But what *happens*?'

'Well, after the boys look you over, you've gotta get initiated. Then you're one of us, and you can live in the woods like we do.'

Cordie rested her head on the ground. She stared through the lacework of branches at pale and cloudless bits of sky. 'If I join up, they won't kill me?'

'Not if they like you.'

'I have to . . . make them like me?'

'Righto.'

'And then they won't kill me?'

'You'll be one of us. That's how I joined up. That's how a lot of us did.'

'All I have to do is go out there, and . . . What do they want to do, screw me?'

'Sure.'

'So they screw me, and that's it? They won't kill me or anything?'

'Yeah. That's about all. Then we'll take you to the village, see. You'll have to go through some shit there, but it's nothing. Old Grar has to give you the okay, stuff like that. Nothing to worry about. Come on.'

Cordie lay still, afraid to move.

The village, she thought. They'll take me to the village. Maybe that's where Mom and Dad . . .

'Move it!'

God she didn't want to go out there!

'The guys are gonna get tired of waiting.'

'Okay,' she said.

'You first.'

She forced herself to move. She turned around

and began to squirm forward on her belly, head down.

What if Lily was lying?

What if they planned to kill her?

But she had no choice.

She kept inching forward.

Then she saw them. Three of them. Teenaged boys. Squatting naked in the sunlight just outside the bushes, staring in at her.

She stopped, cramped with fear, and looked back at Lily.

'Keep going.'

She shook her head.

'Go on.'

'No!'

'At the sound of crushing foliage she snapped her head forward. Two of the boys were scurrying toward her, smashing aside the bushes in their way.

'No!' she shrieked.

She kept shrieking as they grabbed her arms and dragged her from the thicket.

Chapter Twenty-three

'Why don't they come?' Neala asked, whispering so she wouldn't wake Johnny.

'You sound like you want 'em to,' Sherri said.

'Hardly.' She was dressed and standing in the doorway, watching the distant Krulls. Several times, she had tried to count them. They kept moving, though – some vanishing into the timber, others appearing. She counted twenty, twenty-four, nineteen, twenty-six. They seemed to be doing nothing special. Just milling about. She couldn't see them well because of the crosses and heads.

'It's like they're waiting for something,' Neala said.

'Yeah. For us. Why don't we shut the door?'

'We've got to keep watch.'

'We can,' Sherri said. She closed and latched the door. 'Over here.' She stepped sideways through the darkness, and lifted one of the deer skins draping the front wall. Sunlight spilled through gaps between the logs.

So this is how Sherri spied on us, Neala thought. Anger and humiliation began to burn in her. How much had Sherri watched? The whole thing? Had it turned her on?

God, how could she sink that low!

Reaching up, Sherri yanked the deer skin loose. She flung it aside. 'That's better,' she muttered.

Neala peered through a crack. She could see exactly where she'd been with Johnny. She looked up, saw the Krulls still wandering beyond the stakes, and lowered her eyes again to the spot where she'd made love to Johnny.

'Why'd you do it?' she whispered.

'What does it matter?'

'It matters to me.'

'Look, I said I'm sorry.'

'I know. I don't want another apology. I want to know why. You're my best friend, Sherri. How could you stand here and spy on me?'

'We're all going to die here. You know that, don't you?'

'No, I don't.'

'You think your Johnny will wave a magic wand and – *Presto!* – we're home again?'

'Hardly.'

'Those people out there – those *things* – they're going to get us sooner or later. And it won't make a damn bit of difference why I watched you, will it?'

'It makes a difference to me now.'

'Suit yourself,' Sherri said.

'Tell me.'

'Just let it go.'

'I can't. Not if we're going to stay friends.'

'Shit.'

'Okay. If that's all I mean to you . . .'

'You have no idea what you mean to me. Not the slightest.'

The words frightened Neala.

'I love you.'

She looked at Sherri, stunned. 'What do you mean?'

'You know what I mean. And when I saw you, this morning, standing there in the sunlight . . . I just couldn't help myself. I couldn't stop watching.' She made a sour laugh. 'You probably thought I was hankering after Johnny, huh? Surprise, surprise.'

'I can't believe this.'

'Believe it, Neala.'

'But those guys you're always talking about – Jack and Larry. Wesley . . .'

'Men are okay. But you – I *love* you.'

Neala shook her head. She felt disgusted and afraid.

'I'd hoped we might . . . Never mind.'

'What were you going to do, seduce me?'

'Have I ever? Have I ever *tried*?'

'No,' Neala admitted.

'I'd never do anything unless you were willing.'

'Boy.'

'I'm sorry.'

'All these months . . .'

'Sorry,' Sherri said. She stepped away from the wall. 'This would be a great time for an exit, but I think I'll pass on it.'

Neala watched her move across the room and

lie down in a corner. Turning again to the wall, she peered out the crack.

I love you.

The words were like a heavy stone in Neala's stomach. She felt betrayed. As if her friendship with Sherri had been a nasty trick. Not a friendship, at all, but a game Sherri had played to stay close to her. To sneak intimate moments: a glimpse of her body, a casual touch, sometimes a quick, happy hug.

Her face felt on fire as she remembered their weekend in San Diego, last month. After a day at Sea World, the motel room. Calling to Sherri from the shower because she'd forgotten her shampoo. Sherri's little joke. 'If I was a guy, I'd climb in and lend you a hand.' Not such a joke, after all. A suggestion.

She must've prayed I'd ask her to come in, anyway.

It must've been torture for Sherri.

The whole weekend. Being so close to me but never close enough.

She remembered other scenes from that weekend, now. The times they changed clothes in the same room. The night Sherri gave herself a breast examination.

If she'd offered to perform the examination on Neala, it would've been suspicious. Sherri'd been too smart for that. She'd played the game well.

She hadn't been subtle that weekend, but she'd misdirected Neala like a skillful magician.

'Get a load of this number,' she'd said, pulling a sheer, black negligee from her suitcase. 'Wesley picked it up at Frederick's. Horniest son of a bitch I've ever met.' She'd dropped her bathrobe onto the bed, and slipped into the negligee. 'Cute, huh?'

'What there is of it.'

'Well, it's the only nightgown I've got, kiddo. I just brought it along in deference to your modesty. I usually sleep in the raw.'

'Don't let me stop you.'

Sherri did a lot in the raw, that weekend. Neala just assumed she liked the free, natural feel of it. Now it didn't seem that way at all. Sherri'd been displaying herself, trying to entice her.

Well, she hadn't been enticed.

That must have been terrible for Sherri. The weekend must have been a torment. All the time they spent together, for nearly a year, was obviously filled with pain and frustrated desire and hope. Constant, unfulfilled hope that Neala would finally respond.

God, the misery Sherri had put herself through!

Neala looked across the dark room. She saw Sherri in the corner, lying on her back, an arm over her face.

She went to her.

She sat down beside her.

'My turn on watch?' Sherri asked.

'No.'

'What're they doing out there?'

'Just waiting.'

'Gonna starve us out.'

'Hey, Sherri.'

'Huh?'

'I'm sorry.'

'You?'
'I'm just sorry I couldn't be what you need.'
'Yeah. Me too.'
Neala reached down, and took Sherri's hand.

Chapter Twenty-four

They stripped Cordie. Then two boys held her to the ground while another tried to mount her. She twisted and kicked. He battered her legs away, got between them, and clutched her thighs to hold her still. He thrust against her. The head of his erection prodded, missing, missing, then finding the split of her vagina and plunging in. She cringed and closed her eyes tightly.

'Look at him,' Lily said. 'They don't like it when you shut your eyes.'

She kept them shut. The boy pounded into her with quick, hard strokes.

'You'll be sorry,' Lily warned. 'It's an insult, shutting your eyes. You want 'em to kill you?'

Cordie opened her eyes. The boy's face was above her. He watched her with narrow eyes. His bloody lips were drawn back, baring his teeth. He grunted loudly with each thrust, blowing putrid breath into her face.

She turned away. Lily was squatting beside her, next to the boy who kept her right arm pinned. Another girl, this one chubby but small-breasted, stood behind them. As she watched Cordie, she rubbed herself with the knobby end of a bone. The

bone appeared slippery and fresh. Cordie quickly
looked away, back to the boy gasping above her,
then away from him.

The boy pinning her left hand was younger
than the others. He watched her with eager, wild
eyes. Behind him stood a slender girl with a
stump where her elbow should have been. A
small, dried hand hung round her neck on a
thong, its brown fingers curled as if about to
clutch something.

The boy was pumping harder now.

Cordie stared at the girl's withered hand. She
tried hard to concentrate on it, to figure out
whether it was a left hand or a right hand, to keep
herself from thinking about the boy grunting and
sweating on top of her dirtying her insides . . .

A left hand.

The girl's left arm had the stump.

Therefore . . .

The dried-up thing dangling between her breasts
– was it her *own* severed hand?

The boy suddenly thrust deep and stayed, tight
against her, head thrown back and mouth wide,
his body twitching as he throbbed inside her.
Cordie was sickened by the feel of his jerking
penis, his spilling seed. She gagged.

The boy pulled out of her. He stood, pointing at
his shiny erection and making a comment in a
language Cordie didn't know. Then he stepped
back, hands on hips.

The boy on her right let go of her arm.

Cordie whimpered.

'It's part of the test,' Lily said.

When he was on top of Cordie, about to enter her, she clenched her fist.

'Hit him,' Lily whispered, 'and you're dead meat.'

So she lay beneath him, her free arm tense but motionless at her side, as he rode her to a climax.

He stood, said something to the group, and stepped away. He stood at the side of the first boy, and folded his arms.

The one at her left released her other arm. Cordie glanced at Lily, kneeling close by. Lily was flushed and breathing hard. The girl behind her was writhing on the bone she held in both hands. The one-armed girl stood motionless, her bare skin glossy with sweat, her fierce eyes meeting Cordie's.

Jealous?

She's jealous, Cordie thought. Of me!

The young one climbed onto her. He pushed his penis into her. It was smaller than the others. His mouth went to one of her breasts. Sucked the nipple. Gnawed it. Wincing with pain, Cordie clutched the grass. Then the pain streaked through her. She grabbed the boy's hair and jerked his head away.

He snarled like a raging dog.

Cordie heard a sharp laugh. She glanced at the one-armed girl, and saw a vicious smile on her face.

'You blew it,' Lily said.

The words struck Cordie with sudden, cramping fear. She pulled the boy's face down to her mouth and kissed it. She darted her tongue into his mouth. She stroked his back. She clenched his buttocks, digging into his smooth flesh, pressing him more deeply into her. The boy moaned with pleasure. She eased his head away from her face, and pushed his mouth to her breast. His teeth clamped it, chewed it. She cried out with pain, but kept thrusting against him, kept squeezing his buttocks, and finally pushed a finger into his tight sphincter. He shook with spasms, moaning and gasping as he came.

He looked haggard and pleased when he climbed off her. He pointed to his erection, spoke, and joined the other two boys.

Cordie sat up.

The three boys began to talk. They nodded. They pointed at her.

The one-armed girl suddenly shouted. She jerked her knife out of her skin belt and flung it to the ground. Strange words spat from her mouth.

The boys nodded.

'Tough,' Lily said.

'What's going on?'

'Kigit says you're shit. She doesn't want 'em to let you in. She says you're weak and yellow. Says she wants to fight you.'

'*Fight* me?'

The boys were nodding, agreeing with Kigit. She turned away from them and walked toward Cordie.

'You'd better stand up.'

'I have to fight her?'

'You better try.'

Cordie got to her feet as the girl approached. Her legs felt very tired and weak. She hurt inside from the assaults. Wetness spilled from her, rolling like syrup down her thighs.

She backed away from Kigit. She moved past the side of the thicket, wondering if she dared to turn and run.

Kigit smiled strangely. She pointed behind Cordie.

Cordie didn't look. She wouldn't be tricked. She continued to step backwards until her bare foot slipped on a patch of wetness. She took a quick step, trying to catch her balance, and tripped on an obstruction.

She fell onto her back. Sitting up quickly, she found herself in the midst of severed human limbs. They were scattered all around – arms, legs, two mauled torsos.

Kigit picked up a glob of loose meat and tossed it underhand at Cordie.

She screamed as it landed on her belly. Then she scrambled to her feet.

Kigit picked up a severed arm. She held it to her own stump and waved it in a parody of her own missing arm.

Cordie turned and ran. She heard the girl behind her, drawing closer. She lunged sideways. Leaped over a dead trunk. Darted through bushes that flailed her skin. But Kigit kept getting closer.

Where were the others? The boys? If it's just this girl, this one-armed girl . . .

Cordie plunged forward as Kigit shoved her from behind. She landed hard, facedown, twigs and thorns tearing her flesh. As she started to get up, Kigit pounded onto her back. The weight drove her down. Kigit's arm cross her throat, choking off her wind. Using both hands, Cordie forced the arm away.

They rolled, but Kigit came up on top. Straddling Cordie's chest, the girl shot a punch between her upraised arms. The fist felt like a hammer smashing Cordie's nose. Her arms dropped heavily. Kigit's knees pinned them to the ground. One blow after another crashed against her face. Finally, they stopped.

Though she kept her eyes open, Cordie was too dazed to struggle. She watched the girl above her, grinning down, then leaning forward so the withered hand dangled above her face. The hand lowered. It's dry fingers dragged across her forehead.

Cordie whimpered at the touch of the clawlike hand. She felt the scrape of its fingernails along her cheek. Kigit used her living hand to guide it toward Cordie's mouth. The fingers hooked her lips. They tore. She tasted blood. She felt the nails against her front teeth.

Lily knelt beside her, and she suddenly realized that the others had caught up. They stood in a close circle around her, watching in silence.

Suddenly, Kigit jabbed the dead hand at Cordie's right eye. She jerked her head sideways. The fingers raked the side of her face. Twisting frantically, she worked her arm out from under the girl's knee. She grabbed a breast and wrung it.

Kigit cried out, falling sideways as Cordie pulled.

Cordie kept her grip. She climbed onto the writhing girl, whose single hand battered her arm, trying to free the tortured breast.

Turning, she dug her elbow into Kigit's throat. She put her weight on it. Something crushed, and her elbow punched deeper. The girl bucked, eyes bugging out, mouth agape, arm swinging wildly. Cordie blocked it. She crawled off the convulsing body and got to her knees.

Everyone watched Kigit until she died.

Then a boy, the one who'd been first to assault Cordie, spoke.

She turned to Lily for an explanation.

'He say's you're okay, but you've got to pick up Kigit and bring her along.'

'Where?'

'To the village.'

Chapter Twenty-five

Willis Hogue threw a leg over the counter stool as if he were mounting a horse. 'Give me a coffee, Terk.'

'Where's your trout hat, Hogue?' Terk tapped his own hat, a billowing chef's cap of spotless white.

'Wife's got me over a barrel,' Hogue told him. 'She bought herself a fancy antique mirror, and guess who's hired to hang it up?'

'Ain't me.' Terk poured steaming coffee into a white plastic cup in front of Hogue. 'Must be you.'

'Must be.' Hogue blew on the steam. 'A real tragedy, last night.'

'Yes and no.'

'I was mighty sorry to hear about young Fielding. He was a decent sort. Went to school with my Roger.'

'Can't say I was sorry to hear about Shaw and his brat,' Terk said. 'Or Hank Stover, either.'

'Well now, I'm not one to piss on the dead. And Fielding was a decent sort. It's a shame.'

'Hear about John Robbins?'

'Hear what?'

'Bob Rath stopped in for a Danish; he said

Robbins flew the coop. They went over by his house there on Olive Street, last night – looking to find the ladies, you see. Well, Robbins weren't there. His car, neither. They're thinking he took up with them.'

Hogue blew on his coffee, and took a sip. 'Well, I suspect they'll turn up. Can't get by the roadblocks, and they for sure won't try walking out.'

'Rath, he said they've got a house-to-house search going on.'

'I wouldn't mind being the one that finds 'em.'

'Maybe you can get in on it.'

'I suspect the wife wouldn't approve. She's mighty hot to get that mirror up.'

Hogue left the diner, and stood beside the highway while a Volkswagen whirred past. The young man and woman inside were strangers. Hogue grinned. Probably on vacation thinking, *My oh my, what a quaint little town.*

Hogue rushed across the highway, hanging onto the belt of his drooping trousers. At the other side, he hitched them up and tightened the belt a notch.

'Mornin' Roy,' he called.

Roy, carrying two suitcases toward the motel office, grinned. 'How're you today, Willis?'

'Can't complain. How's the wife?'

'Oh, Rose Petal's as chipper as ever.'

'That's good, that's good.' Hogue continued on his way, walking along the highway's gravel shoulder.

Why a fella'd take up with a gal that old . . .

Well, she hadn't been that old when they got married eighteen or twenty years ago. She must've been sixty, though. A retired hooker, that's what everyone said. Well, one man's meat . . .

Hogue reached the door of Phillips' Hardware. Through its glass, the store looked dim and deserted. Hogue tried the knob.

'Damnation,' he mumbled.

A decal on the glass gave the store hours: Mon–Sat 10 am.–6 pm.' Well, this is Saturday and it's after ten. He checked his wristwatch. Right. Ten forty-five.

He knocked on the door, and waited. Then he knocked again.

'Come on, come on,' he muttered.

'What's the trouble?' Roy called. He was standing beneath his motel sign, still holding the suitcases.

'You know anyplace else that carries Molly bolts?'

'Not off hand. I'm positive Phillips has them.'

'He's not open.'

'Oh, he *must* be.'

'If he's open, he's got a funny way to show it. Door's locked tight as a gnat's asshole.'

'That so?'

'Does he usually open on time?'

'Like clockwork.' Roy set down the suitcases, and approached. His jowls quivered with each step. Hogue wondered where Roy picked up his flowered Hawaiian shirt. Probably from one of his more flamboyant guests.

Roy tried the doorknob, as if he thought Hogue incapable. 'You're right,' he said.

'That comes as no surprise.'

Roy pressed his face to the glass. 'Doesn't look like he's in there.' He pounded on the door, then kicked it twice, shaking it in its frame. The exertion worked up a sweat. He plucked out a handkerchief and mopped his brow. He ran the cloth over his shiny pate.

'You know what this means?' Roy asked.

'Means I can't get my Molly bolts.'

'It means Phillips didn't get here.'

'Maybe he caught a bug.'

'Or a bug caught him.' Roy widened his bulging eyes. 'Maybe a *lady*-bug.'

'What're you getting at, Roy?'

'I happen to know that Art Phillips was seeing Peg Stover on the sly.'

'By George, that's right!'

'Now you take me, I think it's kind of funny he didn't open up today, when you consider what happened last night.'

. 'You've got a point.'

'I think I'll just take a run over to Phillips' place, and see what I can see.'

'I was about to head over that way, myself.'

Roy's eyes narrowed. 'Were you?'

'Why don't we pool our efforts? If we can find the gals, we'll split fifty-fifty.'

'Come along, then. We'll take my van. And Rose Petal. She wouldn't want to miss out on this.'

Hogue waited in the motel office. He fidgeted

while the minutes passed, worried that the house to house search would beat them to Phillips' place. If that happened, he would be out a thousand dollars – half the standard bounty for two defectors.

The door behind the registration desk swung open. Roy came out, lifting the Hawaiian shirt above the white paunch of his belly and pushing the barrel of a revolver into his belt.

'You wouldn't have a spare sidearm, would you?' Hogue asked. 'I'd pay you for the loan of one.'

'This babe's all I've got.'

'I'll want to stop by my place, then.'

'You go on ahead in your car. We'll meet you at Phillips'.'

'Well, never mind, then.' He didn't want to give them a headstart.

Rose Petal came out. She clacked her false teeth at Hogue, and winked a lid bright blue with eye shadow.

'Good morning,' he said.

She saluted by touching the head of a claw hammer to the bill of her Dodger cap, knocking the cap askew. She didn't bother to adjust it.

As she followed Roy around the end of the desk, Hogue noticed how her breasts dangled inside her loose T-shirt. Printed on the shirt front was the word BABY with an arrow pointing down.

Sick, Hogue thought.

When she came around the corner, he thought for an instant that she was naked below the waist. Then he saw that she wore pink bikini pants.

Wait'll I tell Terk about this, he thought.

Hogue tried not to look at her as they left the office and went to Roy's van. She climbed in ahead of him, presenting him with a full view of her scantily clad bottom – intentionally, Hogue suspected. He turned his eyes away.

Inside the van, Rose Petal disappeared. Hogue took the passenger seat.

'It'll still be fifty-fifty,' Hogue said. ''Regardless of Rose Petal.'

'A deal's a deal.'

'Good enough.'

As the van crossed the highway, Rose Petal reappeared. She held a crowbar out to Hogue. 'Skull buster,' she said. Her breath smelled like Listerene.

'Why, thank you.'

Little more than a minute later, Roy parked at the end of a block and shut off the engine.

'Phillips' place is three doors up,' he said.

'I don't think we should just go up and ring the doorbell, do you?'

'That wouldn't get us far,' Roy agreed. 'We need a plan.'

Chapter Twenty-six

Robbins woke up and found Neala asleep beside him on the bed of fur. He raised his head. Sherri was at the front wall, keeping watch.

He gently removed Neala's hand from his belly, and got up. He went to Sherri. 'What're they doing?' he asked.

'Just standing there.'

He peered out. 'What the hell are they waiting for?'

'Maybe they plan to starve us out. Beats getting their heads shot off.'

'Yeah.' He stepped away from the wall, and lifted his T-shirt to wipe the sweat off his face. Then he picked up his rifle. He went to the door and opened it. The air from outside gave no relief; it felt even hotter than the air inside.

'Actually,' said Sherri, 'I think we'll die of thirst long before we starve.'

'We're not gonna do either.'

'What do you plan, mass suicide?'

'I plan to get us out of here.'

'Rotsa ruck.'

He stepped into the sunlight. Squinting he

looked through the weirdly tilted crosses and mounted heads.

Must be two dozen Krulls out there. Not doing a damn thing. Just lounging around, like it's a picnic.

Picnic.

Robbins made a grim laugh.

A few of the Krulls perked up when they noticed him. Some pointed. One young fellow ran forward, stopping at the edge of the pikes, and hurled a spear. Robbins watched it soar, knowing it would fall short. It did. It tore half the face off an impaled head. The head twirled, its black hair swinging behind it.

Angry voices broke the silence.

Two Krulls attacked the boy. They threw him down. They stomped and kicked him.

Because he flung his spear at an impossible target?

Or because he damaged one of the heads?

Maybe the area's sacred, Robbins thought. It would explain why the Krulls hadn't entered.

He walked along the front of the cabin to its corner. More Krulls along the side. He counted eight. They could be re-enforced quickly, though, by some from the front.

He moved to the rear. More there. Thirteen or fourteen wandering idly beyond the barrier of heads.

He gasped at a noise behind him. Swung around. Found his rifle muzzle inches from Neala's belly.

For an instant, she looked terrified. Then a smile came to her face. 'Don't shoot,' she said.

'Wouldn't think of it. What're you doing up?'
She shrugged. 'Too hot in there.'
'It's hotter out here.'
'But you're here. What are you doing?'
'Looking for a way out.'
'Any luck?'
'Not yet.'

She squinted across the field. Wet hair clung to her forehead. Her face was sweaty. The tiny, moist specks below her eyes glinted sunlight. A drop rolled down toward a corner of her mouth. She licked it away, then dried her face with the front of her shirt. She let the shirt hang open.

'Why don't they come for us?' she asked.

'I'm not certain. I think we might be in the middle of a sacred area, or something. They always stop at the edge of the heads.'

'I would've, too, if I'd had a choice.'

'It's more than just revulsion. Has to be. These Krulls think nothing of tearing people limb from limb. They must have a damn good reason for staying out.'

'Like if these are their ancestors?'

'Yeah.'

'That'd be nice for us.'

'Except.'

Neala nodded. 'Except how do we get out.' She leaned against the wall and hooked her thumbs into the pockets of her corduroys. Her throat and chest and belly were glossy with sweat. 'We gonna make a run for it?' she asked.

'I guess we'll have to. We'll wait till after dark, and sneak out. This way, I guess. The crosses

177

aren't quite so close together, back here. If we can manage to crawl through without knocking any down . . .'

'Everybody decent?' came Sherri's voice.

Neala quickly pulled her shirt together and tucked in its front. 'Yeah,' she called.

Sherri stepped around the corner. 'What's cooking?' she asked.

'We are,' said Neala.

'Maybe that's what they're waiting for.'

Robbins didn't smile. 'We're planning to get out of here tonight,' he said.

'How do we pull that off?'

Robbins explained. As he talked, he saw Sherri look toward the heads. She gazed at them. She seemed lost in her own grim thoughts. 'I know it won't be easy,' he said. 'I don't want to go out there, either. We can't stay here forever, though.'

'I think I will,' Sherri said. She tried to laugh. It sounded more like a sob.

'It won't be so bad,' Neala said.

'What it'll be,' said Sherri, 'it'll be fuckin' ghastly.'

'We'll leave as soon as it's dark,' Robbins said. Sherri nodded. 'Which gives us all day to look forward to it.'

Chapter Twenty-seven

'The car's in the garage,' Hogue reported when they regrouped in the alley. 'I couldn't see in any windows, though.'

'Funny Phillips would keep his curtains all shut, like that. But do you know what's even funnier?' Roy asked. 'His doors are locked. Front *and* back. I tried them both. With great stealth, of course.'

'What's wrong with locking the doors?'

'Just this,' Roy said. 'Phillips doesn't lock his house. Never. Doesn't believe in it.'

Hogue nodded. Strange, all right. He let his eyes roam over to Rose Petal. She winked at him.

'Should we go in?' Hogue asked.

'I'm ready if you are.' Roy glanced at Rose Petal. 'How about it, sweets?'

She licked the palm of her left hand, then smacked the hammer against the wet spot.

'What've you got to lose?' Art asked. 'If I don't drive you out, they'll catch you anyway. You've got nothing to lose by trusting me.'

Jenny took a long drink of milk, and set down the glass. 'I don't trust him, Mom. Once he's got us in the trunk, we're at his mercy.'

'How else can we get out of here?'

'Maybe I could hide in the back seat, under a blanket or something so I'm out of sight. That way, I can keep him covered and blast him if he tries any funny stuff.'

'They'd see you at the roadblock,' Art said.

'Maybe or maybe not. If we wait till after dark . . .'

The doorbell rang.

For a breathless moment, Jenny felt the same panic she'd experienced not long ago, when she lost her footing high in a tree and nearly fell.

Her mother looked gray and sick.

Jenny forced herself to take a deep breath. 'Who is it?' she whispered.

'How should I know?' Art said.

She grabbed the damp, wadded handkerchief. 'Open up.'

Art smirked.

The doorbell rang again.

Jenny picked up the shiny automatic and pressed its muzzle to his lips. She saw fear in his eyes. He *knew* she would shoot – she'd done it before.

He opened his mouth, and Jenny stuffed it with the rag.

'Mom, tape his mouth.'

The doorbell rang again as she rushed into the living room. She glanced at the door. It had no peep-hole, no way to look out.

The curtains were drawn across the picture window. She wondered if she dare lift a corner and try to see who was at the door.

180

No. Better just wait, and keep the front covered. The person would probably leave.

She flinched as the knob rattled.

What if he's got a key!

From the kitchen came a crash of bursting glass.

'Jenny!,'

The curtain above the sink puffed inward as the spray of glass hit it. Then the curtain bunched – a hand was gripping it from the other side. It went taut, and the rod clattered down. The curtain dropped into the sink.

A bald, chubby man pushed his arm through the hole in the window. Roy from the motel. He aimed a dark revolver at Peg.

'Nobody move,' he said. His sweaty face was smiling.

Something crashed into the kitchen door. The door shook, but stayed shut.

'Mom!'

Roy's eyes shifted away from Peg and widened. His revolver started to move.

Peg dropped to the floor. She heard two quick flat cracks, then a single heavy *caroom*.

'Mom quick!'

She scurried under the table, and crawled.

The door crashed again.

She shoved a chair out of her way and crawled toward the hallway entrance, where Jenny crouched with the automatic.

The girl fired again.

'It's okay,' Jenny gasped.

Peg scrambled the rest of the way. She dropped

onto the hallway carpet. Looking back, she saw nobody in the window.

Then the kitchen door burst open.

Willis Hogue stumbled in, looking surprised. He backpedaled. Roy, behind him, shoved him forward.

Jenny fired. Hogue's mouth made a tight O. He dropped onto his rump, and stared down at the hole in his stomach.

Roy, standing behind him, aimed hastily and shot.

Jenny cried out.

Peg whirled around, aghast. Jenny's hand was empty. The outstretched fingers trembled violently. The shiny automatic lay on the carpet a yard away, its slide dented and half torn off.

'Reach for the sky!' Roy announced. He stepped over Hogue's squirming body and came toward them, chuckling quietly.

Chapter Twenty-eight

Cordie had little chance to see the village before she was pushed into a hut of branches. 'Stay here,' Lily said. 'Grar has to see you.'

Then she was alone. She sat cross-legged in the center of the hut. The floor was specked with sunlight from the leafy roof. She sighed. It felt good to be rid of the body. But later . . .

She didn't want to think about later.

At least for the moment, she didn't seem to be in danger.

They'd accepted her.

They'd fucked her raw. Kigit had tried to kill her. But she'd done everything right, so far. She was almost one of them.

With both hands, she wiped the dripping sweat from her face. From her shoulders and breasts.

Once they trusted her, she could find a way to escape.

It might take a while. A few days, a week . . .

The pelt over the hut's entrance flapped open, and a creature swung in on hairy arms. Cordie caught her breath. She gripped her thighs, digging fingernails into her wet skin, fighting her urges to flee or scream.

The creature, she realized, was a man. A man of hideous deformity, legless and bloated. His mouth twitched into a mockery of a grin.

'Grar?'

The monster swung closer.

Cordie squeezed her thighs harder. Her fingernails pierced her skin.

Inches from her knees, he stopped. His eyes roamed her body.

No!

Not him!

Watching his gummy eyes, she knew she would die before letting him take her. She crossed her arms over her breasts.

The creature growled.

'No,' she whispered.

Then the fur swung away from the entrance, and a man came into the hut. An old, lean man. He spoke, and the creature scuttled away from Cordie.

'I am Grar,' he said. 'Our companion is Heth.'Your name is?'

'Cordelia.'

The man came forward on hands and knees; the hut was too small for standing. He wore a skirt of hair that hung to the ground as he crawled. It was many colors: brown, red, blond, and raven black.

He sat in front of Cordie and crossed his legs.

'You are one who escaped the trees, last night.'

'Yes.'

184

'I understand that you wish to become one of us.'

'Yes.'

'Why?'

Was the question a trick? She saw no malice in Grar's eyes. 'So I won't be killed,' she said.

'Joining us is no guarantee of that. We have dangers unknown to you.'

She nodded.

'You must give us children,' he said. 'Children to replace the many who have fallen. And you will give us fresh blood to mix with the blood of our fathers. Without new blood, the children come forth weak and crooked, like Heth.' He nodded toward the deformed man in the corner. 'The blood of his parents was bad.'

Too much inbreeding? Cordie wondered. She didn't realize it could create such monstrosities.

'You will give yourself to any man until you are with child. After your firstborn, you may accept those you wish, rejecting others.'

'Okay,' she said.

'Now we must go.'

Her heart slammed. 'Where?'

'To your friends.'

'I don't . . . Who?'

'Those who escaped with you from the trees. You will go to them.'

'I don't know where they are.'

'They have taken shelter in the house of The Devil. You must go to them, and bring them out.'

She stared at him, perplexed and frightened.

'Only you, among us, may enter the land of the dead.'

'Oh Jesus, I don't . . .'

'The women are young. Like you, they will give us many children. We must have them.'

'But there's a guy.'

'You will take his life.'

'Me? Kill him?'

'You have killed others. You killed Kigit.'

'This guy's got a gun.'

'You are a woman.'

'That's not . . .' She stopped herself. Defiance would do her no good – and might get her killed. 'Okay,' she said. 'I'll do whatever you say.'

'I hear deceit in your voice.'

'No. I'll do it, honest. I'll kill the guy. I really will. Then I'll make the women come out.'

'If you betray us, your death will be horrible beyond nightmares.'

In a dry voice, she said, 'I won't betray you.'

'Heth.'

The creature scuttled forward.

'Your hand, girl.'

She raised her left arm.

The old man lightly took her wrist. He guided her hand toward Heth. She made a fist.

'Open your hand.'

Her fingers fluttered open.

'Please,' she whispered.

'You must learn a lesson in obedience,' Grar said, and moved her little finger toward Heth's mouth. The dry lips sucked it in. She felt the

186

edges of his teeth. The tongue stroked the length of her finger.

Then he bit.

She saw her bleeding stump.

She saw Heth chewing. The ceiling of the hut tilted strangely, and went dark.

Chapter Twenty-nine

'What time do you think it is?' Neala asked, staring through the doorway.

Sherri shrugged. 'Cordelia's the one with the watch.'

'I'd guess it's past noon,' Johnny said. 'Maybe one.'

'It gets dark around eight?'

'Yeah,' said Sherri.'That gives us seven hours. Can you die of thirst in seven hours?'

'I doubt it,' Johnny said.

Neala wiped her face. 'I wish night would get here.'

'It will,' Johnny told her.

'And then,' said Sherri, 'the real fun starts.' She lay down on her back, folded her hands beneath her head, and stared at the ceiling. 'Hide and seek with the boogy-men.'

'We can't stay here,' Neala said.

'If we had water, we could.'

'But we don't.'

'Maybe just one of us should go out, tonight, and bring some back. He could fill that pot . . . '

'You volunteering me?' Johnny asked.

'Sure.' She grinned at him. 'You game?'

'Not hardly. By the time I could make it to water, I'd be home free. I might as well keep going.'

'Right! Great idea! Keep going, and get help. Bring in the cavalry. Get us out of here in a chopper, and blow these fuckers to hell.'

Johnny was silent. Neala turned to him, alarmed. 'You're not seriously considering it?'

'Well . . . '

'Damn it, Sherri!'

'Hey, it was only a suggestion.'

'It has some merits,' Johnny said.

'No!'

'I probably could get help. Search and Rescue over in Melville, has a copter. If I get to them, they could set down right outside the door. Only thing is, it would take a while. I'd have to make it to the road and get my hands on a car. My car, if it's working. Then I'd have to make it through Barlow.'

'What's the problem with that?' Sherri asked.

'Barlow? Everyone knows me. If I'm spotted, they'd try to stop me. But Melville's only half an hour past Barlow, so I could get there pretty fast if nothing goes wrong.'

'Yeah,' Neala said. 'If nothing goes wrong. In the meantime, we'd be sitting here alone. No food, no water, no way of knowing if you made it.'

'The thing is, you'd probably be safe here. Out beyond the heads, you'd be vulnerable.'

'Just like you.'

'I can move fast, alone. If I make it, I'd be back by morning with that copter.'

'And if you don't make it?'

'You're no worse off than if you'd been with me.'

'It's a good idea,' Sherri said.

'Hold it. Just a minute, damn it. Johnny, didn't you say it's twenty miles to get out of Krull territory?'

He nodded. 'That's if you head east.'

'What's this *if*? That's the way you led us, last night. East.'

'If I go out alone, I'll head west.'

'Back the way we came?'

'I'll try to get back to my car. If I can get it started . . . '

'The place was *crawling* with Krulls!'

'Last night,' Sherri added.

'Okay, last night. So do you think they just vanished since then?'

Sherri smirked. 'They're right outside.'

'That's right,' Johnny said. 'Right outside. Must be fifty of them surrounding this cabin. That's fifty who aren't prowling the woods. If I can just sneak past the ones right here, the rest of the way should be a cinch.'

'If it's a cinch,' Neala said, 'let's all go together.'

Chapter Thirty

'You've got to believe me,' Art whined. 'I was lying to them. Once I got them in the car, I was going to drive them straight out to the Trees.'

'Aw shut up, you old kickee.' Rose petal squinted at him through the dim light of the van.

'Honest. You've got to believe me.'

'You rat,' Peg muttered.

'It isn't fair!'

'I knew he was lying,' Jenny said.

The van lurched sideways. Peg rolled, her back pressing against Jenny. When it straightened, she rolled away.

She lay on her side, lengthwise on the floor of the van, her head toward the rear doors. Her hands, behind her, were cuffed to Jenny.

Two men had come to the house after Roy called. They'd been rough. They'd jammed on the handcuffs tightly, cutting off Peg's circulation.

They hadn't believed Art.

'I heard Phillips talking,' Roy had told them. 'He said he would drive the gals out tonight, hiding in his trunk.'

It was the one bright spot.

Peg flexed her hands. The numb fingers felt like sausages. She could barely bend them.

'Please, honey,' Art said to the old woman.

Rose Petal glanced toward the front of the van. Roy's bald head was visible above the back of the driver's seat. She looked again at Art.

He was sitting upright on the floor, not far from Peg's feet, his hands cuffed overhead to the handle of the side door.

'I'll give you whatever you want,' he said.

'Money, do you want money? Anything. *Jesus* just don't take me to the Trees!'

Rose Petal crawled toward him.

Peg could see sweat sliding down his face and chest. He blinked it out of his eyes.

'A key!' he whispered. 'Have you got a key for the cuffs?'

Rose Petal got up on her knees. She turned her ballcap backwards, like a catcher. Then she raised the hammer.

Art gaped.

She took a quick glance toward Roy, then swung. The hammer thunked, knocking Art's head sideways. His eyes rolled.

'Mom? What's going on?'

Peg couldn't speak. If she opened her mouth, she might scream. She watched Rose Petal toss the hammer into her left hand, and hit Roy's mouth. The hammer broke through his upper teeth. Blood and white chunks of tooth slid down his chin.

Rose Petal swung again. His right cheekbone collapsed.

As if suddenly regaining enough consciousness to know what was happening, Art screamed. He bucked and twisted wildly. Rose Petal slammed the hammer against his forehead.

He slumped.

The van stopped. Roy swiveled his seat around. 'Oh, for Pete's sake,' he muttered. Rose Petal shrugged.

'Why'd you have to do that, sweets?'

She pointed her hammer at Art's face. 'Asked for a blow job.'

Roy laughed. 'Well, I guess the damage is already done. It's up to you to clean the van, though.' Then he turned forward and the van started to move again.

Rose Petal pounded into Art's skull with the hammer claws. When she started to hack at his eyes, Peg shut her eyes tightly.

She heard pounding, and wet slapping sounds, and sometimes a squeal of surprise and delight from the old woman.

Finally, the van stopped again.

The rear doors opened.

'Holy mother of God!' a man gasped.

Peg kept her eyes shut.

'Get over here, Burt. Look what she done to Phillips.'

'Fuckin' A,' muttered the second man.

'Well, let's get on with it.'

Hands clutched Peg under the arms, and dragged her.

'*You* take Phillips out.'

'Queasy?' Roy asked.

'She's your wife, bud.'

Then Peg was outside the van, a man holding her up. He let go, and she stumbled backward against Jenny. They both fell down.

She opened her eyes. The clearing was brilliant with sunlight. The six dead trees stood in a row. They were taller than she'd imagined. And more ghastly. They looked too much like arms reaching out of the soil, arms picked clean of flesh, their bones smoldering under the sun.

Though birds swooped and fluttered in the bright sky, none went near the Killing Trees.

She and Jenny were pulled to their feet.

A man unlocked the cuff on Peg's left hand. 'Don't make any trouble,' he said in a hushed voice.

At the nearest of the trees, the man fastened the cuff again, securing Peg and Jenny back to back. Without a word, both men walked away. They said nothing as they passed Roy and Rose Petal, who were dragging Art by the feet. They ducked into their car and shut the doors. Then they sat motionless, apparently waiting.

'Well, ladies,' Roy called cheerfully, 'Guess you've met your Waterloo.'

'Sit on it,' Jenny yelled.

'Quiet,' Peg muttered. She didn't want Rose Petal coming at them with the hammer.

They dragged Art's body to the closest tree, and propped his back against it, the crushed pulp of his face toward Peg.

'Have a good time,' Roy said.

Rose Petal waved good bye with her hammer.

Then Roy lifted a shiny whistle to his mouth and blew a high, shrill blast.

As they hurried away, Art's body tipped over. Rose Petal started to come back, but Roy gripped her scrawny arm and pulled her to the van.

The two men in the car followed the van from the clearing.

Peg and Jenny were alone.

Peg shut her eyes. She heard the distant engine, the singing birds, the buzz of flies or bees.

'We'd better get out of here,' Jenny said.

'How?'

'I've still got a knife. The one in my sock.'

'Will it cut steel?'

'Won't have to,' Jenny said. 'Somebody'll come by, pretty soon, and uncuff us.'

'I'm not looking forward to it.'

Chapter Thirty-one

A giant chased Cordie over a barren, glaring landscape of dunes. She whimpered as she ran.

Oh, if he caught her!

His shadow blocked the sun from her body. Such a cold shadow. She tried to run harder, but the sand clutched her feet, slowing her down.

The arms of the shadow reached out.

A monstrous hand gripped her shoulder. Its fingers felt dry as bone.

She bit off its little finger.

Roaring in pain, the giant released her. She ran on, out of the cold shadow, leaving the giant far behind. But she was lost and the dunes were strange. She didn't want to be here, after dark.

Where were Mom and Dad?

They must be nearby. They wouldn't leave her all alone in this horrible place.

She tried to yell, but the giant's finger was still inside her mouth. She pulled it out. How odd! It was just her size.

She stuck the giant's finger onto her stump. A perfect fit.

She began running again, but the finger fell off and disappeared in the sand. Dropping to her knees, she raked through the sand trying to find it.

Ah, here it is!

She pulled, but it was stuck. She pulled harder. Out of the sand came an entire hand, an arm . . .

She staggered back, suddenly afraid.

Someone buried in the sand was rising!

He sat up, sand spilling from his body, and grinned at her. 'Hi, Cordie.'

'Ben? I thought you were dead.'

'Not me,' he said, and brushed sand out of his hair.

No, not sand. Ants.

'Ben!'

He brushed harder His head tumbled off and dropped to his lap and Cordie sat up screaming.

She was in the hut.

Lily sat at her side. 'Nightmare?' the girl asked.

Cordie raised her hand. It was wrapped in a bloody rag. The hand pulsed with pain. 'My finger,' she said.

'Yeah. Well, you're lucky that's all you lost. Grar doesn't trust you much.'

'I told him I'd do it. What does he want! Christ, my *finger*!'

'We've gotta get going. Come on.'

She crawled behind Lily, keeping her injured hand off the ground. The sunlight outside hurt her eyes. Squinting, she got to her feet.

Grar came forward, his skirt of hair floating over his legs. He held a sword. It looked, to Cordie, like a saber from a Civil War movie. He handed it to Lily, and spoke in the other language.

Lily nodded. She turned to Cordie. 'Okay. This way.'

The group of Krulls parted, and Cordie faced the landscape of pikes and heads. She jerked her arm free of Lily's grip.

'Your friends are in the cabin.'

She shook her head. She felt numb.

'Here. This is for you.' Lily held out the saber, hilt first.

'Use it on the guy.' She raised her arm. Saw her hand close around the hilt. The weight of the sword dragged her arm down like an anchor.

'Get going,' Lily said. 'The quicker you get it done, the quicker we can get our asses out of here.' She saw fear in Lily's eyes. 'We don't want to be around when *he* comes back.'

Cordie couldn't move.

Lily pushed her, and she began to walk. The heads seemed to bob and sway in her vision. A bird fluttered down. A black bird. It perched on the nearest head, and pecked a gash in the forehead. The skin split, but no blood flowed.

Something familiar . . .

That face.

Ben!

Chapter Thirty-two

'One's coming through!' Neala said.

Robbins hurried to the doorway. He grabbed his rifle. Dropping to one knee, he took aim. He watched the girl stagger among the crosses, bumping into some.

'She drunk?' Sherri asked.

'Something's sure wrong with her,' Neala said.

Robbins lowered his rifle.

'Well shoot her, for Christsake!'

'None of the others are coming,' he said.

'So what?'

'She looks crazy,' Neala said.

Robbins stood up. He stepped into the sunlight.

'What're you doing?' Sherri asked.

'Just a second.' He ran to the corner of the cabin and checked the Krulls at the side. None were approaching.

'Johnny, what . . . ?'

He ran to the rear, looked beyond the barrier, and returned to the front. 'It's okay,' he said. 'She's the only one.'

'You aren't just gonna let her come, are you? Look at that fuckin' sword!'

'That's just what I'm looking at,' Robbins told her. 'I want it.'

The girl tripped, smashing through half a dozen crosses before she sprawled facedown. She raised her head. She got to her hands and knees. Bracing herself on the sword, she stood. She looked back as if to see how far she'd come. Then she faced the cabin. She squinted, and raised an arm to wipe sweat from her forehead.

The motion lured Robbins' eyes to her breasts. They were large for such a slim girl, and shiny with sweat. Robbins felt a warm rush of arousal. He lowered his gaze to her belly, to her dark wedge of pubic hair.

'Look at that,' Sherri said. 'She's got bathing suit lines.'

Sherri was right. The girl's breasts and pubic area were pale.

'That's Cordelia!' Neala gasped.

Robbins studied the face. It was swollen and bruised and marked with cuts, but it did resemble the girl who'd been with them last night.

'Cordelia!' he called.

Her head nodded slightly.

'Holy shit,' Sherri muttered.

Cordelia staggered forward. She stepped high over fallen pikes, then ducked to pass under the cross-bars of those ahead.

'God, what've they done to her?'

'I think she's in shock,' Robbins said.

She stumbled again, and fell to her knees.

Robbins slung the rifle across his back. He started forward.

'Johnny, it might be a trick.'

'Maybe,' he admitted. He pushed his way through the crosses until he reached her. She was still on her knees. She stared up at him. Her eyes looked wide and blank. He slipped his hands under her armpits, and lifted her.

'It's all right,' he said softly.

She raised the sword high.

'Johnny!' Neala cried.

His hand slid up and gripped her feeble arm.

'It's all right,' he said again.

His other arm circled her back, and he pulled her against him. Pressing her tightly to his body and still clutching her arm, he swung her around and carried her through the fallen crosses.

In front of the cabin, Neala took the sword from her hand. Robbins carried her inside. He lowered her to the floor. Rolling onto her side, she drew her legs up to her breasts. She held them there. Her mouth sucked on her knee.

'Cordelia?'

She didn't respond.

Robbins turned to Neala and Sherri. 'Maybe we'd better just leave her alone for a while.'

He went toward the doorway, Neala at his side.

'I'll stay with her,' Sherri offered. 'she might need someone.'

'Fine.'

They left Sherri beside the girl, and went outside. They found shade at the rear of the cabin. There, they sat together. They held hands, and talked softly. Neala lay on her back, and rested her head on Johnny's lap. He stroked her hair.

When she yawned, Robbins told her to sleep. She shook her head. Her eyes were full of sorrow. 'We have so little time,' she said.

'We'll have years,' he told her.

Tears came. He brushed them from the corners of her eyes.

Chapter Thirty-three

A burly, red-haired man ran out of the timber, a knife held high, its blade flashing in the sun.

Peg pressed herself hard against the tree, as if hoping the dead trunk would envelope and hide her. 'One's coming,' she whimpered.

'Just one?' Jenny asked.

'So far.'

He wore only a belt and an empty knife sheath. His penis swung wildly as he ran.

'My God!' Peg gasped.

'What?'

'It's Chief Murdoch.'

'Lois's dad?'

'What's *he* doing here?' Far behind him two more figures came out of the trees. One was a woman – a pregnant woman, her belly stretched and bulging. The lean, blond man beside her held a spear. 'Two more,' Peg said.

'Four coming my way,' Jenny said.'Oh Mom. Oh geez, Mom!'

Murdoch stopped in front of Peg. He pressed the knife point to her throat.

'Don't get many townies,' he said.

'Charlie . . .'

Richard Laymon

'Always glad when we do, though. I love seeing their faces.' His other hand began to unbutton her dress. 'Always so shocked. What's Charlie Murdoch doing out here with the Krulls?'

'Don't.'

'They started Barlow, you know. Needed a civilized front. Speaking of fronts ...' He chuckled softly, drew the knife down her chest, and cut through her bra. He pushed the cups aside. 'Nice.' He lowered the knife. As he sheathed it, Peg saw his penis rising stiff. Then she felt his hands.

'No, please.'

'What's he doing?' Jenny demanded.

'Shut up,' Murdoch said. Then he spoke softly to Peg. 'Know what we're gonna do to you?'

'No.'

'Thought everybody knew.' His hands left her breasts. They opened her belt. Then tugged the dress. The cloth split down to the hem. Crouching, he gripped both sides of the strip, and tugged. The hem popped apart.

The two Krulls stood just behind him, watching. The man was naked, his eyes fixed on her body, one hand stroking his erect penis. The pregnant woman wore something like a bikini on her swollen breasts. Only not of cloth.

Of skin.

Peg felt Charlie's hands slide up her legs. They hooked her panties and dragged them down.

Faces!

The rags of flesh on her breasts were faces. Small, oval faces. The faces of children!

208

Peg shut her eyes tightly.

She gagged, but stopped when Charlie yanked her legs out from under her. The tree scraped her back. She thought her arms would tear from their sockets. But she didn't fall far. She opened her eyes only long enough to see her legs hooked over Charlie's shoulders. She felt his mouth, his flicking tongue.

'*No!*'

'What are you doing to my mother!' Jenny cried. 'Stop it! Damn you, I'll kill you!'

Then a fat, female Krull hurled a spear at her. It thunked the trunk above her head.

She watched the four approach. Among them, only one looked normal: a boy no older than herself. He was blond and naked. For an instant, she thought he was Timmy. Then she remembered what she'd done to Timmy. She was glad. If she got a chance, she would do the same to this kid.

The others, though . . .

The fat one who'd thrown the spear was hairless and white. Her dead-white skin was shiny and slug-like.

Another woman hurried along behind them. She hobbled, bent low at the waist like a speed skater, one arm twisted behind her back. Her young face was distorted as if fingers were pulling it to one side. Her long breasts hung low. Her knees bumped them as she rushed forward.

The last, a wild-haired man, skittered through the tall grass like a lizard, powerful arms driving him forward, his legs dragging behind him.

Jenny cringed as her mother shrieked 'No! NO!'

Then the boy reached Jenny. He slipped the knife into the neck of her blouse, edge outward, and jerked. The blouse ripped open.

'Oooo,' moaned the fat one. She shoved the boy aside, and spread the blouse, and pressed herself against Jenny. Her skin was slick and sticky. She licked Jenny's mouth. Her hands opened Jenny's pants.

Jenny drove her knee into the soft belly. The girl fell away, gasping. The boy laughed at her.

Now the bent woman came in close. She nuzzled Jenny's belly with her face.

Jenny tried to knee her, but the lizard man had her ankles.

The bent woman sighed, licking Jenny's belly. Then she bit.

The lizard man bit her thigh.

The fat slimy girl, up again, kissed her and squeezed her breasts.

She screamed into the fat girl's mouth.

Chapter Thirty-four

Neala opened her eyes. She was lying on her side, her body against Johnny, her face touching his bare chest. She felt as if she'd been asleep for a long time. A breeze moved over her skin in warm, fluttery waves.

There had been no breeze, earlier. With a start, she rolled onto her back. The cabin's shadow stretched a long distance. 'Oh God,' she moaned. She turned to Johnny. 'It's so late, she said.

'We've got a couple more hours.'

'I don't want you to go. Not without me.'

'You'll be safe here.'

'I don't care if I'm safe. I want to be with you.'

'Well, we'll see. I just . . .'

'Hey guys!' Sherri called through the wall. 'You'd better get in here.'

'Right in,' Johnny said.

Neala sat up. She didn't look toward the wall. All afternoon, she had kept her eyes away from it. If Sherri was spying again, she didn't want to know.

She and Johnny got dressed. They hurried to the front of the cabin and entered its open door.

Cordelia was sitting up.

'She wants to tell us something,' Sherri explained.

'Yeah,' she said. 'It's what they sent me in here for. You're supposed to come out.'

'Surprise, surprise.'

'They won't kill you if you come out.'

'Sure,' said Sherri. 'I'll just bet.'

'No, it's true. They'll take you in. You can join with them. They won't kill you.'

'Why not?' Neala asked.

'They need you . . . They've got too much inbreeding.'

'They want us for making babies?'

'Yeah.'

'What about Johnny? He's hardly capable . . .'

'He can come, too.'

'Stick to the truth,' Johnny warned.

Sherri turned to him. 'You know what she's talking about?'

'I know they'll accept women, sometimes. Young ones. Pretty ones. For recreation. And for breeding, I suppose. That may be why they don't want the Barlow people fooling with them. They don't take men, though.'

'Is that true?' Sherri asked Cordelia.

The girl nodded.

'You mean they'd kill Johnny?' Neala asked.

'I suppose.'

'You bitch! What're you lying for!'

'I'm sorry,' Cordelia whispered. She held up her left hand and plucked a filthy rag away from it. 'See what they did?'

212

Neala glimpsed the stump, and looked away.

'One of them bit it off. As a lesson. To show what they'd do to me if I didn't get you two to come out.'

Sherri laughed once, harshly. 'This sounds like a great outfit. First they fuck us, then they bite off our fingers.'

'And they kill Johnny,' Neala added.

'Thanks, but I'll pass,' Sherri said.

Cordelia looked up at each of them. 'If you don't come with me, you'll all get killed.'

'They can't get to us here,' Johnny told her. 'If they could, they wouldn't have sent you to talk us out.'

'It's not them. It's . . . someone else.' The fear in her eyes chilled Neala. 'I saw him last night,' she said. Her voice lowered to a hoarse whisper. 'He killed Ben. He put Ben's head on a pole. He put all these heads on poles. They call him The Devil, and they won't come to get you because this is his cabin, and he's coming back.'

'When?' Johnny asked.

'Maybe tonight.'

'She's trying to trick us again,' Sherri said.

'No, honest. He's real and he's – horrible!'

'We were here last night,' Johnny said. 'He didn't come then.'

'He was out killing. He killed Ben. He would've killed me, but I hid.'

'If he comes,' said Sherri, 'we'll just hide.'

'You're crazy. He'll kill you all.' She pushed herself to her feet. 'I'm going back. I'll tell 'em you aren't coming out.'

'Don't go back,' Johnny said. 'Stay here. We'll all get out.'

'Oh no you won't. I've seen . . . I've seen *him*. I'm going back.'

She stepped unsteadily toward the open door.

'Cordelia, don't.'

'You're fools,' she said. She pointed through the doorway. 'Your heads'll be out there by morning.'

Her sword was propped beside the door. She reached for it.

'Leave that here,' Johnny said.

'Okay,' she said.

Then she grabbed it, whirled around and attacked.

Chapter Thirty-five

She drove the blade toward Robbins' chest. He was sitting on the floor. It should have been easy.

But in the few steps she took to reach him, Neala dived at her legs, Sherri scurried toward the fireplace, and Robbins dropped backward. She kicked through Neala's arms and lunged at Robbins. His leg swung up. It caught the blade. Crying out with pain, he threw himself sideways. The leg of his jeans held the blade. She lost the sword.

Sherri swung the fire poker at her head. She blocked it with her forearm. Neala sprawled on the floor, grabbed her left leg and bit into her calf. As she tore loose from Neala, Sherri swung again. The poker's black point whipped past her eyes, just missing. She turned and ran. At the door, the poker slashed. It ripped down her back. She raced for the forest of pikes, Sherri close behind. The poker *whushed*. Missed. A skull leered at her. She ducked under the cross-bar. Falling to her knees, she scrambled forward.

She looked over her shoulder. Sherri had stopped.

Neala appeared in the doorway with the rifle.

She aimed and fired. Dirt and twigs exploded from the ground beside Cordie.

She lurched forward, plowing through a dozen crosses before another shot blasted the stillness. She threw herself down.

Something under her belly. She knew, without looking, what it had to be. With a gasp, she rolled off it. Her back hit a pole. She froze.

Nothing fell.

Lying on her side, panting, she could still feel the touch of what she had fallen on. She shut her eyes tightly, and reached down. With the back of her hand, she knocked it away.

Then she lay down flat again, and waited for the next shot.

It didn't come.

Finally, she looked back. Sherri and Neala were gone.

She pushed herself to her hands and knees. Ahead, through the tilting bars of many pikes, the Krulls waited. They were silent. All seemed to be watching her.

She remembered Grar's warning. *If you betray us, your death will be horrible beyond nightmares.*

They can't get me here, she thought.

She lowered herself to the ground. She cushioned her face on an arm bruised by the poker, and shut her eyes. The ground felt good beneath her, in spite of the scratchy twigs and weeds.

She would stay here.

Though the breeze was mild, the sun baked her

back. Sweat slid down her skin. Sometimes, she felt the tickle of insects. But she didn't move. It would hurt to move. And it would do no good, because there was no way to escape the heat or bugs.

No way to escape the pain.

Or the Krulls.

No, this is how to escape the Krulls.

This is how.

This . . .

Then the terrible heat was gone. She opened her eyes, and saw that dusk had fallen.

Many of the Krulls were gone. Many remained.

Maybe when darkness comes . . .

No.

If she left, they would find her.

Do unspeakable things. *Your death will be horrible beyond nightmares.*

She lowered her head, and closed her eyes.

This is a good place to be.

A good place.

Chapter Thirty-six

'Johnny, no.'

'Here, give me the rifle.'

'You can't make it.'

'I can try. You two hold out as long as you can. If I don't get back with help, go on out to the Krulls and make the best of it.'

Sherri handed the rifle to him.

Using it as a brace, Johnny pushed himself to his feet. He hobbled across the candle-lit room. Sweat poured down his back. Neala saw that he was putting no weight on his bandaged leg.

'Johnny . . .'

'Once I get to the car, I'll be okay. It'll just take longer than . . . the rifle slipped in his grip. He winced and fell.

Neala rushed to him.

'It's okay, it's okay,' he said.

'No, it's not.'

He planted his rifle butt and started to push himself up. He gritted his teeth. He blinked sweat out of his eyes. His body trembled.

Neala took hold of his arm. 'Wait. Just sit down and rest for a minute. Please.'

He lowered himself.

'Here, I'll take the rifle.'

He gripped it.

'I need to go out for a second.'

'Again?' Sherri asked.

She sighed. 'Must be something I ate. Or didn't eat.'

'I'll go with you,' Sherri said.

'Christ, I don't need a guard.'

'Okay. Well, hurry.'

'Be right back.' She kissed Johnny lightly on the mouth. Then she went out the open door. She walked quickly to the rear of the cabin. The gibbous moon hung low over the distant trees. She wished it weren't so bright.

Propping the rifle against the cabin wall, she stepped out of her corduroys. She took Johnny's key case from a pocket and slipped it into the front of her panties. Then she took off her shirt.

The breeze had died soon after dark, leaving the air still and warm. In spite of the warmth, she shivered as she picked up the rifle. She put the sling over her head. The rifle sapped against her back. The sling tugged at her shoulder. It crossed her body, its wide leather strap digging into her right breast. She adjusted it so it passed between her breasts. Then, crouching, she made her way toward the pikes.

'Neala!'

Sherri's voice. Glancing back, she saw her friend run at her.

She rushed for the crosses, but Sherri grabbed her by the hair, yanked her to the ground, and dropped onto her. She grunted in pain as the rifle

220

rammed her back. Sherri clutched her wrists and pressed them down.

'Let go of me, damn it!'

'You want to go off and get yourself killed!'

'Get off me!'

'No. I can't. I can't let you do it, Neala.'

'If I don't go, Johnny will try.'

'We can stop him. Between the two of us . . .'

'Sherri, for Godsake, don't you realize? We can't stay in this cabin. We'll all die. Even if the Krulls stay away, even if this *devil* never comes, we'll just die in there.'

'We could give up, and live with the Krulls.'

'Sure. Only what happens to Johnny?'

'Yeah, I know.' She stared into Neala's eyes. 'You love him, don't you?'

'Yes.'

She let go of Neala's wrists and gently stroked her face. 'Oh Neala,' she whispered 'Oh Goddamn it Neala. Don't forget me, huh?'

'Wha . . .?'

Sherri's fist swung down. It struck the side of Neala's head. She saw the other fist come down, and tried to block it, but she couldn't get her arm up fast enough. The fist hit, rocking her head.

The weight of Sherri's body left. She tried to raise her head, but couldn't. She felt drunk, powerless to control her movements.

Sherri pulled the rifle sling away from her breasts. Rolled her. Pulled the rifle away. She flopped onto her back again. The ground felt much better without the hardness of the rifle.

Sherri, standing like a giant above her, quickly stripped.

'Don'.'

Sherri slung the rifle onto her back.

Neala raised her head. 'Don',' she said again.

'Oh Neala.' Sherri crouched beside her.

Neala concentrated on her arms. They felt heavy, as if she held a large stone in each hand. But she forced herself to lift them. She felt the girl's big hands slide under her and raise her off the ground. She felt the breasts brush lightly against her breasts, the mouth push against her mouth. She hugged Sherri as hard as she could. Then Sherri forced her down.

'You and Johnny stay put,' she whispered, 'till I get back with the cavalry.'

Her fist smashed down.

Neala tried to open her eyes, but couldn't. She tried to lift her head, but the muscles of her neck wouldn't work.

Not even when she heard Johnny calling.

Then he was above her.

'Neala? Neala, what happened? Where's Sherri?'

She found that she could open her eyes. 'Gone,' she managed. 'Went . . . for cavalry.'

A minute passed before she was able to get up. She put on her shirt. 'I was going to go,' she said. 'I stripped, you know, so I'd look more like one of *them*. But Sherri stopped me. She . . . Oh my God!' Neala pushed her hand into the front of her panties. 'No! Oh Johnny!' She pulled out the leather case.

'My keys.'

'I took them while we were bandaging you. I forgot . . . When she . . . She just *attacked* me, Johnny. I couldn't . . . Oh God, what'll she do, now?'

He shook his head. 'If she makes it that far — well, she'll be fairly close to the road. She can hitch a ride. As long as she doesn't get picked up by Barlow people . . .'

'She hasn't got a chance.'

'Sure she does. She's got as good a chance . . .' He didn't finish.

'As we do,' Neala finished for him.

'Let's get back inside.'

She fastened her pants. Johnny struggled to stand, using the fire poker as a staff. Neala helped him up. He leaned on her, and they slowly made their way to the front of the cabin.

As Neala shut the door, a single gunshot blasted in the distance.

Her eyes met Johnny's.

He said nothing.

Chapter Thirty-seven

Peg clenched her teeth, determined not to cry out as she burned with the boy's penetration. Jenny, suspended from a tripod beside her, was still unconscious – had been since the ordeal at the Trees. Peg wanted her to stay that way.

Didn't want her to see all this.

The way the men took turns.

The other things . . .

She shut her eyes tightly, squeezing tears from the corners as the boy thrust harder. His cock felt like a fiery log. They all did, now, all burned her as they plunged and battered.

So far, only four had used Jenny. Thank God the girl was unconscious, except for the first – the boy at the Trees.

Jenny sucked in a sharp breath as the boy tugged at her madly and throbbed.

Then he left her alone.

She swung by her tied hands, her legs too weak to hold her up. She looked down. Her legs shimmered in the firelight, dark with blood.

She looked again at Jenny. The girl's head was still down. Her body hung limp from the rope, swaying slightly. This time, the blood was her own. From half a dozen bites. Her screams . . .

But she wasn't dead. Peg could see the slight rise and fall of her chest. Unconscious, but not dead. Maybe it would be best if she never woke up.

'The ghoul-haunted woodland.'

Peg swung sideways, and looked at the man suspended from the tripod to her right. Until now, she'd thought him dead.

'Beasts,' he said. 'Foul, loathsome beasts.'

'I wish they'd kill us,' Peg said.

'Oh, they will. But first they'll have their sport. Last night . . .' He lowered his head.

'What?'

'They had my . . . my Ruth. They . . . oh what they did! *Bastards!*' he cried out. '*Bastards!*'

Several Krulls near the main fire looked back at him. A big man stood up. Peg recognized him as Murdoch.

'Problem?' Murdoch asked through a mouthful of food.

'You bastards!'

Murdoch came toward them. He took another bite from the forearm he carried.

'Bastard!'

Murdoch grinned. 'I know your problem, bud. You're hungry. Well, we've got plenty to go around.' He pushed the severed arm toward the man's face. 'Help yourself.'

The man kicked wildly, but Murdoch spun away. 'How about you, Peg?'

'Go to hell.'

'Don't worry, it's no one you know.' He raised the hand to her breast. She cringed at its touch.

226

'Get away!'

'It's tender and tasty. The best meat of all. The Krulls, they've always known that. Been eating it for generations.'

'Yeah, and look at them.'

'Oh, that's not their diet's fault. That's from their pet. Just a little radiation. Mixed up their genes a bit.'

She watched him bite the arm and rip a chunk from it. He smiled as he chewed. 'Delicious,' he said, the food muffling his voice.

Then he spit it in her face and turned away, laughing.

'Ghouls,' the man muttered. 'They . . . last night . . . my Ruth. They . . . they *ate* her! Ate her! Right in front of me! Forced me . . . Pinched my nose so I had to open up, and . . . OH!'

The man began to croon softly and mumble.

Peg glanced at Jenny.

Still out, thank God.

'They left the head,' the man muttered, suddenly intelligible again. 'Don't eat the heads. Save 'em for the pit. Oh, the pit! Wait'll you . . .'

'Shut up,' Peg snapped. 'Goddamn it, just shut up!'

'It lives in the pit,' he mumbled. 'You'll see.'

'Shut *up*!'

He went silent.

Peg stared at the patch of darkness. It wasn't far away. A dozen yards, maybe less. Before night had come, she'd seen that it was a hole in the ground. A wide hole. She'd noticed that the Krulls stayed far from its edge. She'd seen them throw in bones.

'That's why they're here, you know.'

'I don't want to know!'

'To feed it. One told me so. To feed it. To keep it happy.'

Chapter Thirty-eight

Cordie, lying belly-down among the impaled heads, heard the insane roar. The same roar she had heard last night. It came from far in the distance.

But she knew he would soon arrive.

Bringing new heads.

And he would find her.

She raised her head. Beyond the pikes, the open field looked deserted. The others must have run when they heard him.

My chance!

They'll all be hiding!

But if they catch me . . . Better *they* get me.

At least she'd stand a chance, out in the woods. Maybe she could find Mom and Dad, and they'd escape together.

She glanced back at the cabin.

They might let her in, if she begged.

No. That's the worst place to be, even worse than here in the heads.

The door couldn't keep him out.

And they didn't have the rifle, anymore. The big girl, Sherri, must have taken it. She'd seen Robbins and Neala come back to the door without her. Then, she'd heard a gunshot far away.

Somebody got Sherri.

Good.

The bitch had really hurt her with that poker – would have killed her if she could.

Good riddance.

The bitches deserve whatever they get. If they'd only come along with her, they'd all be safe now.

She looked again at the moonlit clearing. Again, she saw no Krulls. She'd better not go that way, though. The roar had come from that direction.

So she turned to her left, and began to crawl. She moved slowly, careful not to bump the poles. When she reached a pair too close together, she squeezed through on her side, her back rubbing one stick, her breasts brushing the other.

There were so many! They seemed endless.

But she kept moving, kept crawling, kept dragging herself forward.

Until a quiet sound stopped her.

The pop of a breaking stick.

She dropped to her side and looked back.

Him!

Stabbing across into the ground near the place where she'd entered, so long ago.

How long had he been there?

As she watched, he raised a head high and rammed it down. It made a wet sound.

Then he entered the field of crosses.

He glided through them, turning silently, never bumping a single cross.

Cordie watched, afraid to move.

How could he travel so fast, and not knock the heads off?

He *is* the Devil!

Suddenly, he turned toward Cordie.

He'd seen her!

She heard a tiny whine in her throat. Warm liquid spurted down her thigh.

Then he turned away.

She moaned, and watched him move through the last of the heads.

His awful voice bellowed, 'Krull!'

He kicked open the cabin door.

Chapter Thirty-nine

Neala flinched as the door crashed open. She pressed her face tightly against the deerskin beneath her, and wished she could burrow in.

Heavy footfalls came toward her.

No!

She gritted her teeth, trying not to scream.

'Krull!'

Her body quaked, shaken by terror.

Oh Christ, we should've run!

Any moment, he would fling aside the skins that covered her.

Hail, Mary, full of grace; the Lord is with thee; blessed art thou among women . . .

From his hiding place behind a draping deerskin, Robbins watched the tall dark shape stride toward the far corner.

Across its back, a rifle hung by a sling.

My rifle?

Poor Sherri . . .

The sword clacked against the wall.

The creature swung around. It stood motionless. Robbins held his breath. He gazed at the thing, and shuddered.

233

Its wide, leathery face looked red in the candle light. One eye was gone, its socket a dark slit as if the lid had been torn away. The remaining eye seemed to glare at Robbins with contempt.

Then it lowered to the stack of skins near Robbins' feet. Robbins looked. He saw Neala's hair. Inches of it curled from beneath one of the skins, glossy in the golden light.

The creature lunged. It grabbed Neala's hair and jerked.

The head came free.

It swung slowly as the single eye studied it.

Robbins staggered from behind the deerskin. With both hands, he swung the saber. Its blade struck, lopping off the outstretched arm. The arm dropped to the floor, Neala's hair still gripped in its hand.

He swung again, this time hitting the neck. The saber hacked through. The head tipped sideways, blood spouting. It toppled. A strip of muscle and flesh stopped its fall, and it hung at the chest, swinging slightly.

The body dropped backwards.

Neala, hidden in the far corner, heard the struggle. Thrusting aside the deerskins, she saw the thing standing headless in front of Johnny. She saw it fall.

Later, Robbins unknotted Neala's long, soft hair. He pulled it from the jawbone of the old head, and tossed the head outside.

Among the crosses in front of the cabin, he found one more sturdy than the others. On it, he impaled the head of The Devil. He propped it near the cabin door.

'Robbins!'

Turning, he saw a man moving through the barrier. The thin, pale man casually pushed aside the pikes as he came forward.

Neala took hold of Robbins' arm. He saw that she held the rifle.

'I come in peace,' said the man.

He stepped out of the crosses. A skirt of hair floated about his legs as he moved. He stopped in front of Robbins.

Robbins stared at the moonlit face.

'August?' he muttered.

The old man nodded.

'It's August Hayer,' Robbins said to Neala. 'He's . . . he's the mayor.'

'In the woods, I am called Grar. I am chieftain of the Krulls.'

'Jesus H. Christ.'

'You have slain the devil Weiss.'

'Weiss!' Robbins whirled around. He studied the face of the grim, severed head. 'Can't be.'

'Oh, it is. He's been marauding for years, slaughtering us without mercy. All these heads . . .' Hayer swept a hand across the landscape of impaled heads. 'He was responsible. Our people are primitive and filled with superstition. They called him The Devil, and shunned his cabin. He might have killed many more of us, but for you. With his death, you have purchased your salvation. You shall come with me to the village, and become one with us.'

'That's not good enough,' Robbins said. 'We want out.'

'I'm afraid that's impossible.'

'Is it?'

'We cannot have you leave the woods.'

'Afraid we'd spill the beans? Tell the world about your game?'

'It's hardly a game, Robbins. If you knew the reason we're out here, why the Krulls are here . . .'

'I don't give a damn about reasons.'

'Perhaps you should. If you knew what's at stake. . . .'

'I'll tell you what's at stake. Your ass.' He grabbed the rifle from Neala and jammed its muzzle against Hayer's chest, knocking the old man backwards. 'You're gonna lead us out of here. We're going to my car. You know where that is? Good. Any trouble from you or any of your goddamn Neanderthals, and I'll blow a hole through you so big you can drive a bus through it!'

'You're a fool, Robbins. I'm offering you . . .'

'I know what you're offering. I'm not buying.'

'What about your friend?' He nodded toward Neala.

She glanced at Robbins. Her eyes were still raw from crying over the death of Sherri. She looked dazed and weary.

'I don't think Neala would go for it, either.'

'For what?' she asked in a monotone.

'Total freedom,' Hayer said. 'A life of idle pleasure, at one with nature . . .'

'You've seen those freaks,' Robbins said. 'Do you want to live with them?'

'I'd rather die.'

'There it is, Hayer. Get moving.'

'One more item. You have a sister named Peg, and a niece – Jenny, I believe.'

Robbins' stomach went cold and tight.

'You wouldn't want to leave the woods without them.'

'Where are they?'

'In the village, of course. Eagerly awaiting your arrival.' Hayer removed a ring from his little finger and held it out.

Robbins took the ring. He looked at it in the moonlight and touched the smooth oval of its jade. 'Peg's,' he muttered.

'We'd better go with him,' Neala said.

'Yeah.' Helpless rage suddenly shook him. 'Yeah, take us to the village.' He rammed the muzzle into Hayer's belly. The man doubled, clutching himself and wheezing. 'Take us to the village,' Robbins muttered. He slammed the rifle butt into Hayer's shoulder, knocking him to his knees. 'Take us to the village,' he said, and drove his boot into Hayer's face.

Chapter Forty

'Cordelia!'

She lay facedown among the crosses, watching. She didn't move or reply.

'Cordelia!' Robbins yelled again. 'I know you're out there. Get your ass over here.'

She shook her head, and said nothing.

'I'm not going to hurt you. Now come on. This is your only chance. Weiss – that Devil of yours – he's dead. That means the Krulls aren't scared of this place, anymore. They'll come right in after you.'

She got up on her knees.

'We have a hostage here. We're going to the Krull village. Your parents might be there. We're going to the village, then we're getting out of here. So come on!'

'Do you promise,' she called, 'not to hurt me?'

'If I wanted to hurt you, I'd leave you here.'

'Okay. Okay, I'm coming.'

Chapter Forty-one

Jenny heard a terrible scream. Mom? No, this time it sounded like a man. She raised her head.

Krulls all around. Moving silently in the firelight. The lizard man. The bent woman. An awful thing without legs. And others. So many, many others. Most were gathered around the big hole.

The man kept screaming. He was among them, somewhere. She couldn't see him.

She looked sideways. Her mother still hung there.

But the man who'd been on the other side of Mom was gone.

It must be him.

The screaming stopped. A bunch of Krulls broke away from the group. They carried arms and legs toward the high, blazing fire. One big man – Chief Murdoch – carried the man's middle. Near the fire, he threw it down among the arms and legs. No head was there.

The Krulls stepped back from the hole. They all seemed to be watching it. In the space between two of them, she could see part of the hole.

And she saw the man's head on the ground near its edge. It wobbled for a moment. Then a dark

241

thing squirmed in its hair and snatched it into the hole.

The Krulls all stared.

Nobody made a sound.

Then she heard Murdoch's voice. 'Shall we give it another?'

He was talking to Mom!

He turned to the Krulls and spoke in their language. Then he turned again to Jenny's mother. Pulling out his knife, he took a step toward her.

A gunshot blasted the stillness. Murdoch's legs collapsed, and he fell facedown.

Jenny spun herself around. Near a hut, she saw four people standing in the darkness.

'Okay Hayer, tell them all to stay put. The ones behind us, too.'

The old man spoke in the same strange language Neala had heard him use in the woods to keep the Krulls from attacking. As he spoke, Johnny glanced from Cordelia to Neala. 'Go on,' he muttered. 'Hurry.'

Though breathless and shaking with fear, Neala didn't hesitate. She ran forward with the saber. She tried to keep her eyes on the girl suspended inside the tripod, but she couldn't stop herself from looking toward the Krulls. Some were moving, now, as if recovering from the surprise of the gunshot.

Hayer continued to talk, but she heard mumbling among the Krulls.

'Quick!' the girl called.

With a sideways glance, she saw Cordelia running toward the tripod where the woman hung.

She saw a legless thing swinging its torso through the mob. The one she'd seen on the road, so long ago. It had a knife clamped in its teeth.

She reached the tripod.

Someone yelled.

Jerking her head sideways, she saw a spear punch through Cordelia.

Neala swung the saber high, severing the rope. The girl fell.

'Fucking bastard!' Robbins shoved the muzzle against Hayer's neck and pulled the trigger.

Pivoting, he flicked the lever action and shot the nearest Krull.

Then he limped toward Peg.

Toward the attacking crowd.

Jenny, on hands and knees, glanced toward her mother. She saw a dozen Krulls scurrying toward her. Saw Uncle John staggering toward them, shooting. But a bunch were coming up behind him.

'Uncle John!'

She looked around. The woman who'd cut her down was already running away, running toward Uncle John with the sword high.

Jenny got to her feet, and ran the other way.

A boy with a knife leaped onto Johnny's back. Raised a hatchet. Neala slashed, knocking off his hand.

She swung the saber into a woman's face, whirled, and split the head of a crawling man.

A knife seared her side. She drove her elbow into the face of the girl who'd done it. The girl fell backwards. Neala drove the sword down into her belly.

Someone jumped onto her back. She sprawled onto the girl's body. Felt a blade at her throat.

Robbins punched his rifle to the man's ear and fired. Then he dragged the body off Neala.

He glanced toward Peg. A legless creature, at her feet, was taking a knife from its mouth.

He aimed and pulled the trigger.

Click!

Peg kicked. Her foot caught the legless thing in its face. Flapping its arms wildly, it fell backwards.

But there were so many more!

She twisted and kicked as they approached.

Then she saw her daughter.

'Jenny!' she cried.

The nearest Krulls looked. Turning away from Peg, they began to shriek with alarm.

Jenny ran.

A slithering Krull grabbed for her feet, but missed.

Others reached for her. She was too quick.

A spear nicked her leg, but she kept running. Just a scratch. It barely hurt. Nothing hurt except her hands.

Only one Krull still stood in her way.

Blocked her way.

The fat, slimy one from the Trees. And she looked scared. She tried to duck out of the way.

Jenny shoved the fiery branch into her face. The girl screamed and fell backwards into the pit.

The huge, blazing branch followed her down.

It started with a deafening shriek.

Neala pulled her saber from the chest of a Krull and pivoted, ready to strike at another – but every Krull stood motionless, gaping toward the pit.

Those nearest the pit started to run. Dark cords whipped around the feet of some, and jerked the savages screaming into the hole.

Then every Krull was hurrying away – most running, others dragging themselves along, some scuttling through the village like giant, clumsy spiders.

Jenny stomped on the wrist of a big, legless Krull on the ground in front of Mom. He growled in pain, and his hand opened. Jenny reached for the knife.

Her charred right hand wouldn't work.

She grabbed it with her left, and shoved it into the creature's eye.

A hand clasped her shoulder.

She swung around, slashing, but missed.

'Uncle John!'

'Give me that.'

He took the knife. Reaching high, he sawed through the rope that held Mom.

Both fell.

But the other woman came. The one with the sword.

Something lashed Jenny's foot. Yelping, she jerked away and saw a dark, snakelike thing curl around the throat of the legless Krull and drag his body toward the hole.

The ground near the hole's edge seemed alive with shimmery tentacles.

'Let's go, let's go!' Uncle John yelled.

Then they were all rushing away.

At the edge of the village, before entering the forest, Jenny turned around. 'Look!' she cried. 'It's out!'

'My God,' gasped the woman with the sword. 'What *is* it!'

The four of them stared. 'What have we done?' the woman whispered.

'Survived,' Uncle John said. 'Let's get out of here.'

They hurried through the woods – swam across the stream. Along the way, they rushed past many Krulls. Some cowered in bushes, others scurried up trees as if to seek safety in the high, hidden branches. None attacked.

They ran past several bodies. At first, Robbins didn't understand. He crouched to inspect one. The woman's throat had been slashed. She still gripped the bloody knife.

'Suicide,' he said.

As they crossed the open field, he looked toward the Killing Trees. He saw movement along their pale, bare branches.

Neala stopped and pointed.
'I see 'em.'
Three dark shapes suddenly dropped from the trees, crashing through limbs, slamming into the ground.
'Come on,' Robbins said. 'We're almost there.'

Neala gazed into the darkness around the car, and saw no Krulls.
None inside the car, either.
She sat in the front seat.
Peg and Jenny climbed into the back.
Johnny slid the key into the ignition – the key that Sherri had forgotten to take, couldn't have used, anyway, because . . . He turned it, and the car started.
Later, on the highway, Neala flung her sword from the window. She watched it curve through the darkness and disappear into the foliage along the roadside. Then she slid across to Johnny. He put an arm across her shoulders, and smiled.

QUAKE

Richard Laymon

'IF YOU'VE MISSED LAYMON, YOU'VE MISSED A TREAT' Stephen King

Twenty minutes before the quake hits, Stanley is ogling a pretty female jogger through his living-room window. He ogles Sheila every morning and that's not all he'd like to do to her. The quake might just give him his chance.

When the quake hits, Sheila's husband and daughter are stranded on the other side of the ruined city. The power lines are down, the emergency services can't cope and the evil and the lawless have already begun to comb the ruins. Now Clint and Barbara must make their way home to Sheila, trapped naked in the bathtub in their ruined house. But will they get there before Stanley, the fat pervert for whom the earthquake is a heaven-sent opportunity?

FICTION / HORROR 0 7472 4806 0

Island

Richard Laymon

'This author knows how to sock it to the reader'
The Times

When eight people go on a cruise in the Bahamas, they plan to swim, sunbathe and relax. Getting ship-wrecked is definitely not in the script. But after the yacht blows up they're stranded on a deserted island. Luckily for them, their beach camp location has fresh water and fire wood, and there's enough food to last them out.

Just one problem remains as they wait to be rescued – they are not alone. In the jungle behind the beach there's a maniac on the loose with murder in his heart. And he's plotting to kill them all, one by one . . .

'A brilliant writer' *Sunday Express*

'In Laymon's books, blood doesn't so much drip, drip as explode, splatter and coagulate' *Independent*

'One of the best, and most underrated, writers working in the genre today' *Cemetery Dance*

0 7472 5099 5

HEADLINE
FEATURE